NEUTRAL EVIL)))

LEE KLEIN

Set in Mrs Eaves XL with LaTeX.

ISBN: 978-1-944697-82-2 (paperback)
ISBN: 978-1-944697-83-9 (ebook)
Library of Congress Control Number: 2019952095

Sagging Meniscus Press
Montclair, New Jersey
saggingmeniscus.com

"... conscious once again of the desire and almost the strength to consecrate his life"

—Marcel Proust

"Who makes the Nazis?
Buffalo lips on toast, smiling ...
Who makes the Nazis?
Benny's cob-web eyes!
Who makes the Nazis?
Bad-bias TV ...
Who makes the Nazis?
Intellectual half-wits ...
Who makes the Nazis?
Long horn
Long horn breed"

—Mark E. Smith

On March 18 in history

In 37, Roman Senate proclaims Gaius Julius Caesar Augustus Germanicus ("Caligula") emperor

In 1068, an earthquake in the Levant and Arabian Peninsula kills 20,000

In 1190, Crusaders kill 57 Jews in Bury St. Edmunds, England

In 1325, Tenochtitlan is founded on an island in Lake Texcoco in the Valley of Mexico

In 1813, an apparatus for making coal gas is patented

In 1877, President Rutherford B. Hayes appoints Frederick Douglass marshal of Washington, DC

In 1881, Barnum & Bailey Circus ("The Greatest Show on Earth") debuts in NYC

In 1902, operatic tenor Enrico Caruso becomes first well-known performer to make a record

In 1921, the Chinese Steamer "Hong Koh" runs aground, killing 1,000

In 1922, Mahatma Gandhi sentenced by British magistrates in India to six years in prison for civil disobedience

In 1925, F5 tornado strikes Missouri, Illinois, and Indiana, killing nearly 700

In 1940, Mussolini and Italy join Hitler and Germany against France and Britain

In 1942, FDR authorizes the War Relocation Authority, which oversees internment of Japanese-Americans

In 1945, 1,250 American bombers attack Berlin

In 1952, the first plastic lenses for cataract patients are fitted (in Philadelphia)

In 1965, Rolling Stones fined £5 each for public urination and cosmonaut Alexey Leonov becomes first person to walk in space

In 1967, "Penny Lane" by The Beatles reaches #1

In 1989, a 4,400-year-old mummy is found in the Pyramid of Cheops

In 1990, twelve paintings worth $500 million are stolen from the Gardner Museum in Boston

In 2013, 98 people are killed and 248 injured throughout Iraq

In 2017, on the fifty-eighth day of Trump's presidency, on what would have been John Updike's eighty-fourth birthday, a man who tries to take a soldier's gun is shot dead at a Paris airport, Chuck Berry dies at age 90, and the preeminent minimalist drone/doom band visits Philadelphia

NEUTRAL EVIL)))

JEWS ON TWITTER had placed three open parentheses and three closed parentheses on either side of their names, appropriating a tactic anti-Semites used to indicate Jews on Twitter. My father's side is Lithuanian Jewish so I placed three closed parentheses after my name, with none before it thanks to my Polish Catholic mother. At night I put on my reading glasses, tucked myself into bed, and willfully exposed my senses to an onrushing stream of information and insights about the new administration. The more I devoured my feed, the more I started to think that the best use of my severely limited free time would be to start making plans to assassinate the president. I told this to a younger woman at work who I know spends a ton of time online and she said it'll be easy for you, you'll be able to walk right up to him and shoot him in the face because you're a white guy. She's half-Jewish too. I said my privilege as a tall, white, blue-eyed, well-educated, lower-upper-middle class, cis-gendered male will *finally* come in handy. We laughed about that old Eddie Murphy bit on Saturday Night Live where he wears white face and discovers that, when only white people are around, everything is free. I'd just need to shave, get a fascist haircut, wear my wedding suit and wingtips, take the train to DC, take a cab to the White House, tap on the windows of the Oval Office, and then say *hey can I come in a sec*? They'd see a tall white male in nice suit, wingtips, a fresh fascist haircut. I'd march in, and before anyone could shake hands, all smiles, I'd fill the president full of lead.

Overexposure to my feed made me dream of assassinating the recently inaugurated President of the United States of America but then I decided I had to deactivate my account because I had started to consider my thoughts, whenever I stopped to notice them, tweet-worthy or not. I deactivated my account because I'd started rating thoughts for potential impact, and this branding of my consciousness—best thoughts no longer first thoughts but most liked and retweeted thoughts—was not something I could support or laugh about in some ironic post-anti-capitalist way, not able to understand it's a game and I should play it like a game, a self-marketing platform mostly about marketing Twitter itself. The more you increase your so-called reach the more you increase Twitter's value, and what better way to increase mutual value than by branding your thoughts, what no company has ever laid a claim to in the history of humanity.

I'm too sincere and sensitive for social media, needing hundreds of thousands of characters to get my point across, to build up to it, state it, repeat it, undermine it, evolve it, and associate it with what comes next, following instinct and intuition as it unfurls in longest-form improvisational elaboration, whereas the Twitter/Trump alt-reality would condense everything to come about the night of Saturday, March 18, 2017 into a character-restricted witticism that at best would receive some favorites before it's washed away in the ceaseless progression of explicit and implied arguments for impeachment, which in my case induced a need to move the process forward, expressed most conveniently by lowering my thumb to favorite as many anti-Trump tweets as possible. The number of favorited tweets listed on my profile tripled in the first weeks of the new presidency (reaching more than four thousand before I deactivated my account). My desire to end it all for everyone and move the news cycle forward was emphatic, insistent, the best course of action, yet impossible to actualize beyond an untweetable thought, something I sensed everyone had on their mind too. Just because desire seems impossible to fulfill doesn't make it go away, not at all, not in the least, and so I obsessively favorited tweets, a proxy intervention for now, visualizing one fine day I dressed up, rode the train to DC, and restored a sense of rationality to the world, for example a world in which the head of the Environmental Protection Agency respects scientific consensus on climate change.

The Angel of Death in dry-ice form will seep closer, the end of everything will seem nigh, and in this emotional and psychological environment, I will see a guitarist perform cunnilingus on electricity itself. For now, before I describe this phenomenon, I should say that I've been feeling better, tightening up, training for the ten-mile Broad Street Run on May 7. Ran 6.2 miles on Friday after work and then that night at home with Mamou (daughter's pet name for her mother) and our daughter Kali (her real name is similar but doesn't characterize her as well) we watched a Disney movie, total toothless pabulum from the '90s, legs like stones, unable to move so well but feeling better, not drinking at home anymore.

Everything had gone haywire in the fall, all systems jammed. I shivered in bed, shook, tremored from anxiety, in a way that next time I notice it with any frequency I'll get myself checked out even if I feel like it's seasonal but also somewhat situational. Our home situation is stable, my work situation is stable, our daughter's development upwardly undulates toward personhood with occasional dips in the sine curve thanks to bouts of feral behavior, eating cat food (dry) or spitting her own food out and mashing it into a pie and then eating that, but this too shall pass, or so we hope. She won't be seventeen, spitting out globs of half-chewed pizza, mushing it on a paper plate, achieving preferred consistency, and then eating that as her friends (if she has any) post images of her on whatever social media reigns in 2030, but for now I'm trying to get things back in order, get back in shape in every possible way.

I'd been drinking fancy craft beers purchased from the bottle shop near the pre-school, seven or more dollars every other day on two or three beers to savor at dinner and/or after our daughter goes to sleep, watching hoops otherwise comatose, intentionally self-medicating, semi-aware what I was doing with fancy craft beer. With the change of the season came the porters, the hoppier IPAs, the Great Lakes Nosferatu at 8%, blood red when held to the light, a thick autumnal beard grown out and old favorite hoodie sweatshirts retrieved from summer storage, the seasonal instinct to insulate against the coming winter addled by the all-out anticipatory anxiety of the election (the future of the free world at stake, that's all), the impossibility of one candidate not disqualifying himself over infractions, transgressions, violations, abuses, defilements, debasements, and deceptions that obviously disqualify someone for president, not that any of it mattered—sexually assaulting women didn't matter, generalized racism didn't matter, imitating a handicapped reporter didn't matter, not paying taxes didn't matter, threatening to use nukes didn't matter, suggesting a new American brand of old-fashioned pre-WWII fascism didn't matter, gesturing toward the inevitability of war with China, North Korea, Iran, and an entire religion didn't matter. None of it mattered for sixty-something million American voters, three million fewer than those who voted for the other candidate, the sane and experienced one, and then after the Electoral College results and inauguration and first weeks of his reign it felt like the country had died and been reborn as an unrecognizable version of itself, its worst aspects galvanized, in power, empowered, unabashed xenophobes and outright racists installed in the West Wing, advising the president, a buffoon, a liar, lacking in anything approaching integrity, not that any of it matters when the upper Midwest isn't doing so well economically because not enough white factory workers shifted to tech jobs and related services.

All of it almost cartoonish, a parody, thousands of protesters shaking their fists at an evil overlord atop a black tower in the heart of midtown Gotham, a reality show I watched rapt with the world for the first weeks until it became clear that the real mechanisms of government, including legislation and impeachment, wouldn't move at the pace of Twitter or even an old-fashioned television series. The president's tweeting became charged as his approval rating plummeted, he accused the former president of wiretapping his campaign, and the only thing I wanted to tweet was fuck these fucking fucks, for fuck's sake, put them out of their fucking misery and do us all, the entire fucking world and the future of unborn fucking humanity, a huge fucking favor.

I was reminded daily of a tweet I saw by a writer/editor who on the Wednesday morning after the election tweeted "Godspeed the assassin," an audacious tweet rapidly deleted, worthy of the title of a novel, that reminded me of Godspeed You Black Emperor, an instrumental band from Montreal whose dramatic cinematic surging crescendos evoke geopolitical gloom, ideal soundtrack for our orange emperor on the toilet at dawn tweeting inane assertions that shake the world, unleashing in response an avalanche of serious, well-considered insights and rebuttals and proclamations and presentiments of consequences most dire for our Tweeter in Chief.

Whenever I touched my phone at work or when I sat oblivious with Kali as she played in her bathwater, I read Lawrence Tribe, the Harvard Law professor I had read in a Constitutional Law class more than twenty years ago in college, or a Californian in Portugal who goes by the name Elliott Lusztig, whose profile picture shows a bald-headed, fierce-faced Zinedine Zidane of Real Madrid, a pseudonymous commentator who always seemed to put things in perspective, suggesting the inevitable downfall of the current executive branch, evoking a sort of dystopian optimism, all while I looked at my phone as it streamed to a cheap Bluetooth speaker on the sink the electric guitar improvisation I had recorded in the morning in the basement, oblivious to my child playing with the water running into her bubble bath, all because at the top of the Twitter pyramid there somehow stood a fuckwit.

The shaking subsided but I wasn't doing better until sometime in January when I started building a distance-running foundation on the treadmill at lunch and whenever possible after work, unconcerned with pace, the TV switched off in front of me, a playlist of fast songs* I put together shuffling at high volume, inner thighs moisturized to ward off the great demon Chub Rub. Last year's running was undermined by allergies or bronchitis that never quite went away and ultimately developed into pneumonia around Christmas. My mother demanded I go to the doctor, commanded me as only a mother can, so I went on the Monday after

* "Ice Cream" by Battles, "Slags, Slates Etc" by The Fall, "Kinski Assassin" by Ariel Pink, "B.O.B." by OutKast, "Super Going" by The Boredoms, "Click Click" by The Wedding Present . . .

Christmas weekend and was diagnosed with walking pneumonia but more so my weight was higher than it had ever been and my bloodwork returned with extremely high numbers for Hb1Ac (blood sugar/diabetes) and triglycerides. My bloodwork came back problematic although the doctor had laughed that the Monday after a long Christmas weekend might not yield the best results. That morning I had eaten crumbs from cookies we took home from my parents' house that seemed like pure sugar and chocolate, not thinking it would affect my bloodwork because I didn't expect bloodwork. With antibiotics, the pneumonia cleared up as I read in bed for three days, including Virginia Woolf's *The Waves*, astounded by its attentive phrases, the affirmation of life, and mid-morning on the last day of the year I received a Google notification that The New Yorker's primary literary critic James Wood had included a translation I was lucky enough to see published by New Directions in July as one of his four favorite books of 2016, which flooded my spirit with therapeutic endorphins, what a way to end the year, and then finally on New Year's Day night, days after starting antibiotics, as I lay on my side about to fall asleep, I felt a pure breath like a beam of light cast into a dark cave, a ray of pure refreshing breath cast into the unwell cavity of my body.

For the first time in what felt like almost a year I could breathe deeply again. Walking home from work that first week of January 2017 I inhaled and held cold air inside my chest that felt like a new skill, the novelty of breathing deeply again. For a year I'd been breathless and because of breathlessness couldn't run all summer and missed the seasonal upswing in my health, the expected annual flow of vitality and strength that arrives with warmer temperatures and outdoor exercise. The trip to the doctor revealed terrible numbers, ill health quantified on a form delivered via e-mail, and so I decided to make some changes.

In the kitchen with Mamou as Kali at the dinner table watches her $30 tablet smeared in yogurt, before I leave for the Sunn O))) show on Saturday night, I open the little Tupperware container I keep in the fridge and then I open a square-shaped baggie, three by three inches, with a cookie in it. I also retrieve a little blue lollipop that I put into the built-in change pocket inside the right pocket of my jeans. I then eat a chunk of cookie, maybe a third of it, surprised and pleased by the taste of chocolate.

I so rarely leave the house at night, content to read and sleep and wake early and try to write in predawn silence, but walking alone on the street now, early on a Saturday night but nevertheless after sundown, there's a pervasive whiff of threat in the air, as though melting snowcaps on the sidewalks lend everything an unfamiliar menace. What awaits unsuspecting pedestrians through the fog?

Earlier, on the way home from a late-afternoon trip to the Cherry Hill Mall, somewhat temporally disoriented because we hadn't yet realized we hadn't yet changed the clock ahead in the car, Mamou said *you'll get fucked in the ass if you go out tonight, if you're not careful.*

On the way to the show, passing the bar I used to pop into more than once a week, sometimes even with the frequency I now go to the gym, where I'd sit by a window and read, sipping two or three half-price happy-hour craft beers, a place I rarely visit anymore, I remember the lollipop and open it. I'm already feeling the cookie or maybe I'm just experiencing the novelty of being out alone on the street on a Saturday night.

Someone takes a piss on a storefront, huddled into the door frame. I want to ridicule this young drunk white dude pissing on the door of a new store called South Fellini that specializes in ironic local T-shirts—one features linguini covered in red sauce below "Legalize Marinara;" one reads "WWJD" below an image of Sixers legend Julius Erving AKA "Dr. J"; another shows

Edgar Allan Poe, who near here in 1849 was arrested for public intoxication after getting so drunk he suffered hallucinations and attempted suicide before spending a night in Moyamensing Prison, the penitentiary that once stood where there's now a supermarket and massive parking lot a block north from where the drunk guy pisses on South Fellini's doorframe. I suppose I've conspicuously pissed like this at some point in my life. I only remember a time in Honduras when I had been drinking white rum on a dinner of crackers while watching the sunset and reading Kafka's *Amerika*. I relieved myself on a huge pile of dried palm fronds across a dusty narrow street from what turned out to be the police station and then had to wield quick slurred Spanish to talk my way out of a night in jail. Somehow that was twenty-two years ago now.

My lollipop is surprisingly hot, an unexpected cinnamon flavor almost too much for me, probably to keep children from ingesting it. Blue food items never taste like cinnamon. A blue lollipop that tastes like cinnamon creates sensory dissonance, a cognitive disconnect between sight and taste, an inversion that fits I suppose the trickster profile of an edible, what they call orally administrated THC, a relatively new delivery mechanism for me, although I've consumed marijuana in brownie form before of course and whenever I've chewed and swallowed raw, unprocessed buds I've been surprised by how effective, even mildly hallucinogenic, it's been, and how long the results have lingered.

On the way to the train I pass a guy who vapes a huge cloud that I assume to be weed but could have been whatever foul sweet flavor he loaded into his electronic charger, like a cross between a pen and a flask, absolutely modern yet unappealing despite the supposed pulmonary benefit as a nicotine delivery system (smoking has always been about dominion over fire and maintaining an easily fulfilled desire—the need for a cigarette standing in for elusive existential longings). The vaper passes me on the sidewalk as I head toward Broad Street and almost say something to underscore camaraderie like "I got a lollipop," assuming his cloud includes traces of THC.

I wear a yellow knit hat with an orange ball atop it, a blue down jacket, black jeans, old black leather boots that won't make it to next winter thanks to holes developing on the left toe and side. My beard's growing back after shaving it three weeks ago before a meeting in New York for work. Before going out I dabbed the back of my neck and my beard with inexpensive vetiver oil, something I started using after I liked how it smelled on Kali when Mamou applied it to her feet since it supposedly calms hyperactive kids. At work it also might conceal the scent of a man sitting in a small office all day and maybe calm me too. I first heard of vetiver when I heard the band Vetiver, who I've seen twice. Such comfortable music, like brushed cotton, the hills and fog along the northern California coast, redwood mulch underfoot transformed into sound reminiscent of the ranch-dust Americana essence of The Byrds and The Dead, less like either of them really than edgeless pulp (in the best possible way: no attitude, no ego, the news of the past simmered and thickened into healthy organic mush).

Vetiver I also associate with the previous summer seeing an old college friend on drums with a hugely popular rock band. In my old car as we drove from the Mann Music Center to a bar in Northern Liberties, I was like what is that attractive scent you're wearing? And he was like oh that's just a little vetiver oil I put on after the show. A scent approved by such a man seemed worth a try. He seemed totally self-realized, doing exactly what he wanted to do, touring the world, rocking huge crowds, performing at the highest level, totally seeming to thrive. Positivity and fulfillment and vitality lit his eyes, a great golden god for now in the form of a half-Haitian/half-Jewish, 6'4" powerhouse drummer.

After descending the steps at Broad Street and Tasker Avenue to the train station I'm aware of graceful arcs of iron set out for riders to lock their bikes. Something about the wheels of the bikes there and the iron arcs resemble leaping porpoises. I'm aware at once that this perception indicates the rising effect and efficacy of what I've ingested. I use my keycard and descend another level to an empty platform, suggesting I missed the last train by a few minutes. *You'll get fucked in the ass if you go out tonight*. I think about what she said, what an unusual prophecy, a joke out of nowhere ("sweetness, I was only joking when I said . . ."). What does it mean *to get fucked in the ass*? Mamou said it like she were only a vessel some higher power temporarily possessed to intone an inevitable future occurrence, although I'm sure it was less prophecy than joked expression of her desire for me to stay home since she's leaving on Monday for Vegas and will be there all week. Very out of character, on Friday night, she came to me where I read (Paul Beatty's *The Sellout*) in bed and affectionately suggested I should see the Sixers/Celtics on Sunday afternoon if I wanted to go. She would watch the Creator/Destructor since she'd be away the next week, forcing me to assume all child-rearing responsibility, which isn't an imposition since I love the rhythm we establish whenever it's just me and the kid on our own. Most nights after helping Kali fall asleep I read or watch basketball on my own cheap tablet before falling asleep early anyway.

Now, out in the world on a weekend evening after dark, sufficiently caffeinated, I'm alert. The platform tiles are institutional coral green, the color of urinal cakes. The pillars offer places to hide from echoing voices. I try to act naturally and extract my phone from the front pocket of my jeans and scan musical instruments for sale on Craigslist, seeing if the effect pedals and twelve-string acoustic I posted earlier in the day appear on the first or second page of items offered. I don't have the clear plastic Ray Ban-style readers I found on Amazon for $10 that focus otherwise blurred text whenever held any higher than my navel. Anything lower than my navel I can read just fine, and my distance vision works too, but last year, right around the time of the Republican primaries, I couldn't focus on text, reading in bed had become too difficult, but cheap 1.5x-magnification readers cured me.

I don't fit the profile for prey even with eyesight going and gray in my hair beneath yellow hat with little orange pom-pom that makes me seem 6'6" in boots. Plus, considering that I've been up since five and spent most of the morning and early afternoon trying and failing to write before driving across the Ben Franklin Bridge and ten minutes into New Jersey, to and from the Cherry Hill Mall, my eyes are probably dark with sleep deprivation and the occupying forces of age, responsibility, and whatever else emanates from my skin thanks to the spiritual incursion of lowest common-denominator family life (Disney movie on Friday night, mall excursion on Saturday afternoon).

I stand behind a pillar, my body angled from the tracks so no one can come behind me and push me in front of the oncoming train, or so something inside me won't, on a whim, shove myself down to the tracks as the train approaches. A few weeks ago at the station I use after taking Kali to pre-school, someone jumped or was pushed in front of the train. The steps to the station were cordoned off by police and shuttle buses conveyed passengers north. If we had left earlier that morning I would have seen something I've always imagined happening to me.

Now a youngish white woman with '70s-style owl glasses walks north along the ribbed yellow strip closest to the tracks. She passes where I lean on the pillar's western side (away from the tracks), facing south, braced against a sudden push toward the train. I feel her lens-enlarged eyes peek at me and see her resist looking at me when I glance up from my phone. This isn't my daily morning commute routine.

The train comes. I survive its approach. I board it and assume my regular standing position in front of the doors that never open on the east side of the train heading north. I lean against the plastic divider between doors and seats, without a book as usual in the morning to keep my eyes off everyone. On my commute, when I do look up, the readers I wear these days let me peer into the faces of those nearest me, their pores, every individual eyebrow hair, the chromaticity of their eyes, leaving everyone beyond ten feet a total blur.

A panhandler apologizes to everyone for interrupting our evening but he could use some spare change or small bills as he is homeless and on the street tonight. He's reciting his speech, the same one more or less all subway panhandlers use, always so apologetic about interrupting everyone, delivering what seems like a prepared address learned at a halfway house or detox or jail. The panhandler who stays toward the center of the train is black, younger than I am, apparently unaware that he's speaking as he speaks. No one takes pity on him. Black teenagers, conservatively dressed like they're heading home after church services, ignore him. He stands where he stands because he's attracted by the conspicuous presence of an older couple who look like French tourists, their skin translucent under the florescent lighting. The Euro tourists disembark at City Hall and weave through the uniformly black occupants of the platform, black women in black burkas showing only their eyes. Eleven years ago when I first explored this city I was irritated by their apparent unwillingness to participate in the general culture, how they moved through the subway stations in disguise, their every human particularity concealed in favor of attention-absorbent anonymity. At first when I saw them I sometimes whistled to myself the theme song to the old cartoon Casper the Friendly Ghost, since in a way they seemed dressed for Halloween in black bedsheets with eye slits cut out. But more recently, more than a decade after moving here, I now know they particularize the city more than most people I see, they differentiate the city more than I do, most definitely, and I've even started to find them sort of sexy, trying to discern their form and even for a moment maintain eye contact as a woman in a burka passes me in the narrow City Hall subway station passageways.

The black women in their burkas moving through the subway tunnels, invariably talking on cellphones, somehow remind me of the mannequins on the Mexican blocks of the Italian Market that are only bottom halves, their upper halves removed, modeling jeans. There's something perverse and sexy about those mannequins that are all buttocks and haunches, rough cuts of human-shaped meat in plastic form hanging from hooks at some satanic Ciudad Juarez butcher shop, the same way these women reduced to eyes in shapeless black fabric seem almost sexy thanks to their inaccessibility. They're like abstractions of womanhood thanks to male religious oppression I simultaneously reject (women should be free) and support as a religious minority (women should be free to choose oppression). After the translucent Euro tourists disembark, I'm aware I'm the only white person on the train pulling out from City Hall. There's a sense that it's Saturday night in the middle of March and people want something to happen more than on a Tuesday morning when commuters are just trying to get to work.

Beggars must have once held out pans like they're taking up a collection. I've never seen a literal panhandler. What happened to the pans? No one handles pans anymore. Instead it's half-mast eyes, swaying gently in the middle of the train car, not holding the steel pole for balance, reciting his spiel again, passengers united in awareness that we're ignoring him, sitting, standing, not searching our pockets for spare change or small bills. The auto-beggar maybe hovers in the center of the train because at first he stood there to wear down the defenses of what he suspected were bleeding-heart Euro tourists but he just goes through the motions now that everyone only has eyes for their devices.

Collapsing into myself, closing down perception of the world around me, it takes an effort to look up. Everything's blended or blurred on the peripheries of my awareness. I should keep eyes down like everyone else has eyes down, or so it seems whenever I glance up. I want to look up and stare and really see, but I'm only going two more stops. *I could give a fuck* I want to say automatically, instinctually, and so I look up and bask in exposure to the inverse of some middle-American Red-State experience, the opposite of an Indiana strip mall outside South Bend with everyone white and overweight in their cars. Here, everyone's black, free range, exposed, either extreme united by girth.

I exit the train at Spring Garden and climb stairs to street level behind a pack of slimy white teenagers who rode another subway car north, in from the suburbs going to an all-ages show on a Saturday night in the city. They're skinny and slouched in hoodies, suffering from post-adolescent excreta: acne, greasy long hair, an aura of moistness most likely thanks to pubes crispy with ejaculate, buttery posteriors, socks slick and offensive to the senses. I've taken the subway to shows at Union Transfer a few times before but it's a longer way to the venue than I remember. Icy snow mounds on the sidewalk, empty lots ready for immediate conversion into internment camps, the street four lanes here, two each way, the buildings squat, more exposure to the elements than where we live. It's like Cleveland over here, with more sky visible in theory, but it's obscured by streetlight halos of fog.

As fluidly and as forcefully as I can I move past a trio of tall black men in long coats up ahead on the sidewalk ("I'm fit and working again/walk down the road in the sun/I make a path through a forty strong gang"). The bar to the right with the neon "bar" sign I've stopped at before shows, clattering talk, assaultive acoustics, six dollar beers evaluated while perusing my phone. I'm no longer interested in six-dollar local independent craft beer and public solitude. Something has shifted. "No longer interested in that," I say aloud and almost step into a street I thought was one-way with traffic flowing north as a car comes from my left heading south.

I've walked around the block for a bat hit before previous shows but there's no need for that now. I have printout in hand as I wait in line to enter the venue. A young black guy wearing a bandana restraining a little afro smiles and asks for anything, spare change, a dollar, pleasantly insistent until I look up and say "sorry, man," obviously stoned now, remembering that I'll be patted down, it's Saturday night and the band plays heavy music and employs satanic imagery and wears robes and once played a show in a Norwegian cathedral dating back to 1181.

Security is extra tight. If something is ever going to happen here the chances are higher with a band like this than with some indie pop fiasco. The head of security I recognize from so many shows over the years at this place and an affiliated bar, Johnny Brenda's, usually the only black guy at the show who doesn't have dreads, older than me, muscular, wears a little fez-like hat, always aware, on edge, patrolling the crowd of slouchy white guys with arms crossed, at most swaying to discordant rhythm emitted on stage. Security I suppose needs to tighten after what happened in Paris. As far as I know Sunn O))) hasn't ridiculed or denounced Mohammed but since randomness is how terrorists operate, imbuing harmless minimalist drone metal concerts with potential horror, extra security is called for, a sign of the times, as is my psychic ease as I pass through security unworried about concealing a mini-Ziploc of marijuana and smoking apparatus. With half a cookie and a lollipop at work in me I go through the entry motions, trying not to breathe on the security guy who pats me down or the young black woman checking IDs who looks over my shoulder as though she can't be bothered to evaluate someone now more than twice 21.

The stamp on my wrist lets me access the back bar area of this reconstituted Spaghetti Warehouse, which is wooden, with a very high ceiling, like a barn converted into a stable converted into a church converted into a restaurant converted into a music venue where now there's something of a crowd. On previous weekend nights since the place opened maybe seven years ago I've secured advance tickets for shows I was sure would sell out only to discover a smattering of indelicate long-haired pale gentlemen sitting around looking at their phones waiting for A Silver Mt. Zion, for example, to take the stage, but there's a decent crowd tonight, mostly younger than I am, mostly wearing black, sitting at tables and looking at their phones. The stairs to the balcony I don't ascend. Instead I climb a few steps to the bar at the back of the main lower-level.

Wobbly rows of humans watch the opener's slow, heavy, dark riffs, a trio, drums, guitar, a female bass player who sings and chants a little too histrionically for my tastes. When the guitarist applies his instrument to his face, eating out electricity itself, it seems like a celebration and a purification ritual conveyed in jagged distorted frequencies, sights and sounds emblematic of the earlier anxiety, the extra charge through my body that I started to notice about two months before the election.

I cut across the room and slide against the southern wall (the stage is west, the bar is east, the entrance is north, the bathrooms are south), all the way to the side of the back bar area, raised maybe three feet above the main floor between soundboard and stage. With the balcony above me, the ceiling is nowhere near as high as in the rest of the enormous room, where it's like a vaulted cathedral, less Gothic Cologne than some fifty-year-old church in Cheyenne. A huge wooden fan revolves overhead like the metal one in the IKEA warehouse, an overhead propeller, a thresher for the open field of my spirit, the procession of days, the 10,000+ daily steps, all the movements to make it through the morning and then from home to pre-school to subway to work to gym (locker to treadmill to locker to shower to locker) to work to subway to daycare to home to make it through the evening and back to bed, the routine so ingrained it's mechanical, able to perform the function required from before dawn until I pass out at night, running now at least a 5K (3.2 miles) on a treadmill on my lunch break. My body is stronger, my mind more than benefitting from a regular burst of endorphins that makes it possible to, at the end of the day, clear the dishes and run the dishwasher and tidy up so I'm not crestfallen by food thrown all over the floor or random toys everywhere when I turn out the lights and retire to the bedroom.

"The lights are on a timer" is something I have to remember and say every night to Mamou as a running joke. The regulation of the off-switch on the main front-room light reflects the mechanization of everyday movements required to hold it all together, maintain employment, excel to a degree that ensures autonomy as an individual contributor under a boss who allows me maximum room to make her look good. I don't get anxious that my employment is endangered because I'm on top of it all, have my arms around it, the sense that there's this mess of a mass of work I can constrict until it's a tight little ball in the palm of my hand. The light is on a timer but of course now the days are longer each day. After a while adjustments are required.

I'm aware of my thoughts in a way that makes me aware that I haven't been aware of my thoughts recently. They've been benevolently suppressed by routine, by action, or whenever they asserted themselves I elevated their status to that of a tweet, but in general I'm now beginning to realize that I haven't been thinking, I haven't had sufficient unoccupied free-range time alone to hear myself think, and now it seems I have an hour or more to myself in a crowd of mostly young men willing to pay $22 to stand and listen to super-loud low-frequency drone-doom minimalist-metal in a converted Spaghetti Warehouse.

I've taken a position against the southern wall of the lower level, close to a short hallway leading in either direction to sizeable, clean, gender-specific bathrooms to the east and west. Ahead of me on the other side of the entrance to the bathrooms there's another riser along the wall that nearly reaches stage right (the left side of the stage if in front of the soundboard), where I've stood recently to watch Swans, Steve Gunn, Bonnie 'Prince' Billy with Bitchin Bajas, Sun Kil Moon. I like the elevated perspective more than the aristocratic view from the balcony where I've semi-recently seen Slint, Ariel Pink, Deerhunter, Kurt Vile, The War on Drugs. I also want to see the crowd, not-yet anonymous torsos with the houselights up, the primarily white male crowd in their twenties and thirties, some wearing sweatshirts emblazoned with skulls, Misfits shirts, others more grungy with a '70s rocker look like Lemmy, like stray motorcycle gang members who shred on vintage Gibson SGs, others older with gray in untrimmed beards wearing wool hats knitted by their wives' mothers and fuzzy sweaters and thin rumpled blazers purchased at outlet stores outside Rehoboth Beach. Stray women in attendance seem like they're here on dates that most likely won't go well.

In the balcony I see from my vantage across the room through a thickening scrim of dry-ice smoke two couples who seem like legit rockers, the men with facial hair embodying 1975, leonine like the cruel pimp in Herzog's *Stroszek*, with two women, one taller and skinnier, pale, gaunt, thick blond Scandinavian Iroquois braids on either side of her head, in overalls with what looks like nothing underneath, and another woman with a harder, more handsome face, stronger features, a well-defined jawline, and thick curls she every now and again flips back with a forearm covered in what looks like a brown-leather jacket with fringe along the arms like wings. She seems to hold my eye for what feels like a minute or more, although thanks to the distance there's no way of knowing if she's looking at me or someone near me or above me or the entrance to the bathroom, or maybe she's watching me watching the two couples standing midway along the northern balcony, thinking they're the representative citizens of the room who make the show feel legitimate because they look like real-deal young virile outlaws more than, for example, the guy three spots over along the narrow balcony away from the stage, a guy wearing an "Unsane" shirt, a middle-aged white guy of medium build and brownish-gray hair who really looks a lot like my friend Gibson. It could be him gesticulating, talking, explaining something, sort of holding court high above the floor of the reconstituted Spaghetti Warehouse now between bands, not that I want to catch his eye and wave and hang out with him since I'm savoring these rare island-like hours of solitude.

So isolated lately, immersed in the family unit, the domestic trio of father, mother, and daughter, not to mention cats, houseplants, appliances, books, records, instruments, all the miscellaneous items we own, so many recently acquired pieces of plastic for the sake of the child's education and entertainment, hibernating through a warmer winter that included a seventy-degree week in February. My only friends still in town are England and Gibson. Everyone else moved away since Kali was born four years ago, particularly two good friends with whom I'd drink immoderately and invariably/inevitably talk about writing, books, literature, life. Now I see that it was preferred for me to focus on family, rediscover playing music, cool it with the recreational quaffing of fancy craft beer at home and whenever out on the town. Now I chew strawberry-orange Trident Layers gum and blow bubbles as big as my head that burst across my beard I then retract and chew some more before blowing another oversized bubble, chewing generously, extravagantly, almost like a jaw workout, as though for the first time figuring out what to do with the novelty of not drinking when alone out on the town at a show, positioned no more than fifteen or twenty feet from a not very busy bar. So tired of overpriced beers, not interested in intoxication or spending an additional $40 (five beers at $7 + $1 tip) on plastic cups of beer instead of a commemorative T-shirt, record, or CD to support the band. I wonder if Sunn O))) will pause mid-drone halfway through the show to introduce band members, including whoever's running the dry-ice machine, salute the opener, say how much they love this city, joke about cheesesteaks or roast pork sandwiches or one of the sports teams, and then remind everyone they have stuff for sale over at the *merch* table and will be there hanging out after the show the way Michael Gira of Swans said something similar, producing unexpectedly affable and approachable stage rapport.

The edibles are proving efficacious. One of my daughter's Sargento cheese sticks I consumed before the lollipop since the guy at the practice space where I secured the lollipop said you need to eat some fat with it for it to really work. What a world: spicy cinnamon lollipops consumed after cheese sticks.

I enter notes into my phone's Notes app and everyone around me must think I'm texting or tweeting, not knowing I'm leaning against the wall entertaining myself, leaving behind a trail of misspelled abstractions to decipher later, breadcrumbs to retrace my thoughts, aware that this could be a novel, as though I'm working on a novel now, conceiving it, recognizing the possibility of one when it appears in the wild, committing once again to fulfilling the need to create text from life and work on it daily and let it sit and work on it and let it sit like bread rising until the dough is ready to cook and consume. Every few minutes I flash open my phone in the dark and thumb something out, auto-SMSing myself.

I feel like that Francis Bacon painting I had in my room in high school and college, a hunter or lost hiker in the swirling primary-colored world of a Van Gogh imitation/homage, now also maybe an adequate representation of the individual in the echo chamber, as I lean against the southern wall of the venue's back bar. I stood in the same spot for Swans over the summer. Soundwaves rippled through the air and I laughed as I held my palm to the vibrating wall. I could even feel the loose fabric around my knee agitated by extreme audio.

Conversations around me begin to achieve the tremolo of laughter. "The tremolo of laughter" I note into my phone, registering the back-and-forth inconstant velocity of surrounding voices. It's like all sound has been sent through a Fulltone "Supa-Trem" pedal with the mix and rate knobs cranked. I stand like Francis Bacon's take on Van Gogh's lone hunter/hiker exposed to Saturday night conversations between two men my age maybe, leaning on the divider between the lower-level floor and the raised bar area. I hear one say "you're really well read" as though they're just getting to know each other. The other says something about adjuncting maybe at Temple where I taught ten years ago after grad school, a long time ago now.

The former Spaghetti Warehouse converted into rock venue with a high vaulted ceiling and enormous wooden ceiling fan begins to fill with dry ice. Representative rocker couples disappear in the fog as I plan my move in advance should violence erupt. If a gunman, a man with a gun, men with guns, women with guns, a single black mother with a machine gun and a bazooka, or an Italian grandmother from the old neighborhood runs into the main room from the primary entrance, pistols blaring, my best course of action would be to get down and move as fast I can into the corner where I'd be out of sight unless she enters from the bathrooms, in which case I would get down and hope she doesn't spray bullets to her right. If she enters from the bathrooms I would strongly prefer that she steps into the room and gets sucked into the gravity of the stage. If she stops a few paces into the room I will get down on hands and knees and make my way to the exit to the northeast and then book it to the front door or another set of bathrooms around the corner, hoping there's an emergency exit that way. But if she comes from that direction and enters the main bar area from the back bar area, I will jump the railing in front of me, scamper up the riser along the southern wall and head toward the emergency exit that skirts stage right, assuming she'd be distracted by all the innocent people available to kill at the bar to the immediate north of the soundboard.

Or maybe it wouldn't be men with guns taking advantage of extreme dry ice to wage global jihad, a lone gun man making a statement about minimalist drone metal, a black single mother making a statement about everything, or an Italian grandmother making a statement about kids these days. Instead it'd be Kali, Hindu goddess of creation and destruction, on a chain around her neck seventy-two shrunken heads of men with identical mustachioed facial features, brandishing a flaming sword in one hand, a full-sized decapitated head in the other dripping blood and gore, her skin a bright and unblemished blue like an indigenous occupant of Pandora, the environmentally endangered planet in *Avatar*, stepping on the chests of those she smites, posing for pictures with her tongue all the way out, her signature look, before she vanquishes everyone in the room too stunned by the spectacle of her appearance to absquatulate post-haste.

For my birthday six weeks ago Mamou presented me with a fabric depiction of Kali like an orchid in homicidal bloom that I hung next to my amplifier in the area in the back of our basement I converted into a cozy little cave for a middle-aged man to rock. I look up at it as I play, the smiling mustachioed heads around her neck, the blue skin, the extended tongue evoking Gene Simmons of Kiss, bass player/"God of Thunder and Rock and Roll" in the first band I ever called myself a fan of as I collected all their records in the late '70s. The fabric Kali tapestry is the perfect decoration for my little serial killer chill-out zone, with the wall behind me when I play covered in two Hieronymus Bosch posters, neither "The Garden of Early Delights." Creation and destruction in eternal round, like light and darkness, life and death, the poles between which existence zaps back and forth.

On a Friday night in November not even two years ago, halfway through a concert by the Eagles of Death Metal, an ironic name that may have attracted sincere terrorists, at the Bataclan theatre in Paris, three men entered with AK47s and grenades and killed eighty-nine concertgoers of a crowd of about fifteen hundred. The survivors escaped through emergency exits, hid in bathroom stalls or under desks in the venue's offices or fell to the ground and played dead. I doubt I would have acted like I've already been killed as so many around me were getting shot.

Dry ice fills the room and mixes with grenade and gunfire smoke, the smell of the slaughtered unintentionally shitting their pants, the enormous wooden fan overhead rotating slowly, obliviously, complicit somehow, not descending to decapitate the gunmen. It's easy to imagine leaping over dividers and sprinting with head low and hands out along the floor to the nearest exit but the likely response would involve crumpling into the fetal position in the darkest, most protected corner of the room, making oneself as small as possible, exposing the least surface area to ricocheting bullets.

The time and place seem right for an attack, a spasm of unexpected violence, a fissure across the surface of a Saturday night with a doom drone band playing that wears monkish robes to minimize their presence and maximize a semi-humorous or at least self-aware and not super-serious medieval vibe (it wouldn't surprise anyone if they lowered a miniature Stonehenge from the lights to the front of the stage in the middle of the show).

I'm not suffering from anxiety, not shaking, standing against the southern wall, leaning with back to it or left shoulder, listening to electronic music of some sort I don't recognize, drums mostly, slow and tinged with malevolence, like field recordings from some neo-tribal technological ritual retreat in the Pacific Northwest, everyone on ayahuasca, leaky pineal glands spurting endogenous DMT, standing against the wall carpeted in thick black corduroy to deaden the sound I suppose. The running helps, eating better, looking forward to a week alone with child as Mamou attends a conference in Vegas, looking forward to a week of single parenthood after a week of snow and vomit forced me to take two half-days from work. I took Kali to school one morning and an hour or so after I made it to the office I received e-mails and calls from her teacher saying Kali was vomiting all over the classroom and I had to come get her (the teacher actually said Kali was vomiting all over "my" classroom; use of the possessive irritated me when I considered it later, as though the teacher seemed to show more concern for "her" classroom's cleanliness than "my" child's well-being), which allowed me to work from home as Kali watched the extraordinary *Kung Fu Panda* trilogy. She was fine, the way you're fine after you expel the contents of your stomach all over someone's couch and carpet and change your clothes to the fresh clean backup pair you keep in your cubby in case you piss, poop, or vomit all over yourself. I restricted her intake to bananas, rice, apples, toast, the so-called BRAT diet, and she behaved like a sick little angel, saying she's fine whenever asked (at first, for almost a year, when asked how she was she'd reply "fire," making us wonder what was going on at the daycare, or maybe it was some new toddler slang). She recovered, spent a day at school, and the next day a storm rolled in, a nor'easter colliding with something wicked rumbling down from Canada. It was forecast to end all life as we know it, burying us under endless layers of ice. Schools were canceled in advance, all in the middle of March after trees started blooming and daffodils and tulips appeared thanks to a string of seventy-degree days in February (I was taught in the late '70s of the twentieth century that the appearance of robins heralded the arrival of spring, but now, in the late-teens of the twenty-first century, robins don't seem to head south for the winter anymore). Mamou worked from home and I tried to work from home but could only manage so much on my laptop because I'm used to three screens and a mouse. One small screen and a trackpad doesn't make what I do all that easy.

Before that, before anyone woke up, before the sun rose, it was just me and a notebook and ice tapping at the window next to the chair newly placed in the bedroom so I'd have a quiet, secluded place to write in the early mornings with Mamou sleeping on the futon in Kali's room in case she wakes up crying in the night or decides to entirely overthrow order in her room or somehow hangs herself from the wires that raise and lower the window shades, also because Mamou goes to sleep much later and doesn't wake up well before the sun rises. I still sleep far to one side of the matrimonial bed, where Kali was conceived, giving Mamou room to return whenever she wants, although at this point I don't want her to return because I want to sit before dawn in the newly established chair by the window and write something new.

The week after the vomit and the snow she would be in Las Vegas for a conference for her work, which I won't go into but which seems on the surface not very interesting but is actually a fascinating business model, an unexpected but obvious blueprint for a company's success. She'll be away all week and so, to compensate in advance for the inconvenience of single-handedly managing our child for a week, I'm listening to drum-based electronica piped over the house speakers, the lights down but not out, the room filling with dry ice and the anticipation of bass notes dropped as low as they can go, heavily distorted and sustained, each note a single steady stream but also rough, granular, emitting sparks like barbed-wire prongs, the overall sound like an electric fence surrounding the amalgamated mayhem of history.

This music isn't for everyone. It's not something you put on at a party, not even at the very end of the party unless everyone's passed out or splayed all around on the floor after you spiked the punch with cyanide. It's something you listen to alone, not in your car driving down the highway, although it could work on solo night drives across Nebraska or west Texas when the moon lights the sky and the road's so straight you cut the headlights until you levitate. But in most circumstances, across most roads, it's not road trip music. It's not beach music unless it's a black volcanic beach littered with jagged shards of obsidian and everything smells like sulfur as a red tide laps at collapsing sandcastles. It's not yacht rock unless your yacht has cannonball holes blown into its side and is sinking thanks to old-timey pirates. It's not surf music although I suppose there's something oceanic about it, tidal, like the sound of fiendish blood-red whales swimming in circles, conspiring against harpoons, or an attempt to sonically represent, using traditional electric guitars and amplifiers, the pressure in the lowest reaches of the Marianas Trench (if Mount Everest were moved to the Trench a mile of water would separate its peak and the ocean's floor), where they say the water pressure is a thousand times stronger than closer to the surface. In short, it's a heavy sound, something for the most part listened to alone, atmospheric minimalism born from the deepest darkest note ever played by Black Sabbath guitarist Tony Iommi, who lost his fingertips in a freak accident in his teens and had them capped with metal.

For the in-utero version of the little person who would ultimately be named Kali upon birth, the best baby name I came up with was Iommi. Mamou, hard at work creating the child inside herself, at most politely considered the name I offered, since it has mythological overtones, sounding like the diminutive of Io, mortal human lover of Zeus, who would visit Io in the shape of a dark cloud and transformed her into a cow to disguise her from a suspicious wife. Io eventually became the first queen of Egypt and Galileo named Jupiter's fourth-largest moon after her. For me the name would be a unique variation of Naomi and, unlike Ashley, Charlotte, or Sophia, every time it was uttered it would evoke Black Sabbath.

In its evocation of Iommi, tonight's headliner's sound makes sense to me with age, the way influences have been reduced and refined to an essential tone exaggerated to extraordinary extent and effect. Reduction and refinement jibe with the closing of the walls, compaction of the trash pile of life these days, employment opportunities limited by salary expectations based on years of experience, the restrictions of matrimony, mortgage, and maternity (caring for a child), the constraints of responsibility and stability, grateful at this point to stand between the black-carpeted walls of a reconstituted Spaghetti Warehouse instead of the trash-compacting walls of neediness, poverty, illness, affliction, disease, intolerance, bigotry, abuse, exploitation, injustice, bias, cruelty, brutality, ruthlessness, atrocity, murder, genocide, on and on. I'm aware of the privilege to overemphasize/dramatize constrictions on middle-age white married educated professional fatherhood, but I see its processes at work all around. One of my oldest friends, for example, the day before the show, when asked about how his brother (13 years younger) was doing continuing to handle significant and several times nearly tragic opioid-related issues that had overwhelmed his family the past three or four years, my old friend said that he, my old friend, is essentially an orphan now. He hadn't spoken to his mother or brother since Christmas and only sees his father at the office where his father who founded the company in the '80s and sold it recently was slowly being pushed out. The story of how this friend became an orphan requires its own novel, something to work on once the first draft of his story, how it appears in reality, settles and seems to end, but for now it's still in progress, something to think about before the headliner takes the stage.

The handsome woman in the fringed coat from the balcony makes her way through increasing clouds of dry ice and those standing in wobbly rows in front of the bar. She passes me and opens her mouth in a silent dragon howl, like she's warding me off, creating room for her to maneuver through the crowd. Or maybe it's a yawn I register for a split second as she moves through eerie artificial cloud, a weird reptilian defensive expression against the admiration of men, or maybe it's just a facial tic? I blend my split-second impression of her into the imaginary terrorist coming from the bar entrance, which in turn I blend into an image of Kali the Destructor with seventy-two identical mustachioed heads around her neck, although no tongue.

She's much shorter than she seemed high above standing in the balcony, now already disappeared through the crowd and into the bathroom hallway area, not that I'm out tonight roaming solo intent on pairing up with short women in fringed leather jackets with yawning reptilian facial tics. I'm not suffering from decreased libido, or I should say that my libido, once indomitable and in control of everything, has decreased, and its attenuation these days comes with decreased suffering thanks to decreased desire. Also, generally, if one were interested in an in-person live-action interhuman encounter that leads to no-strings-attached groping and conceivably intercourse (well-protected, with no chance of conception or STD transmission), I can't think of a worse place to seek and secure such activity than at a Sunn O))) show. The only worse place for a middle-aging man to meet a willing woman would maybe be a Sunn O))) show on a snowy mid-winter weekday night instead of a warming Saturday night in early spring.

Most of the handful of women here (venue capacity = 1200; show hasn't sold out so maybe there are 900 or 1000 people here, a pretty decent crowd that includes maybe three dozen women) are on dates, taken to the show by men most likely. One couple seems dressed up like they went to dinner before the show. The guy thought he should tuck in his shirt and the woman wore a sparkly dress, something appropriate for prom, maybe a little more casual but in the realm of evening formal wear, heels, her long brown silky hair hanging in loose tresses that suggest she spent some quality time with curlers earlier or even went to a salon. They could be celebrating their first anniversary of dating, maybe two or three years out of college, mid-twenties, the guy slightly shorter than the woman in heels, they're both a little woozy from drinks before dinner, wine with dinner, coffee with dessert, drinks from the bar at the back of the venue, and are clearly the best dressed couple in the room tonight. I hope winning this award bestowed by me from a distance, this award of winning best dressed couple in the enormous front room of this reconstituted Spaghetti Warehouse, winning Best Dressed Couple hands down and without a doubt, affords a moment of confidence, solace in advance of the inevitable disgrace of leaving early. Or it's possible that after dinner they smoked some strong weed and bob and weave along the same wavelength as everyone else standing around anticipating extended exposure to sonic doom. This will be a referendum on the couple, on this their first anniversary, a hallowed memorial for the demise of their independence. If they stay through the show, they'll survive; if they go, they won't last until the end of the year. Or it's possible of course that they're married, celebrating their first wedding anniversary with some fine dining and a Sunn O))) show, attending because the band happened to be in town tonight, no other reason, and it sounded interesting, they'd always wanted to see a show at Union Transfer, tonight seemed like a good night for it, simple as that. In which case there's no referendum because it's possible that if they leave they do so to return to the comforts of their shared life and slip into something more comfortable and cozy-up under blankets on the couch and stream any number of amazing serial shows available on demand. Or maybe if they're still only dating, they just want to accelerate the evening so it reaches its inevitable endpoint of six or seven hours of vigorous intercourse, which is how I remember single life, my distant bachelorhood, now married six years, four of those with child, five if you count the forty-two weeks when Mamou was pregnant with our prenatal Kalibird, as though by parallax the post-nuptial years warping my memory of the outer reaches of copulative endurance, as though I'd ever possessed the stamina of Pelletier and Espinoza, the critics in the first part of *2666*, during my bachelorhood. Those years, the majority of my adult life so far, were the inverse progress of a butterfly, bright colors exchanged for the wooly gestative comfort of a cocoon that yields a caterpillar offspring, en route to the larval, pupal form of middle-aged parental existence, the final destination achieved once our Kalibird caterpillar of a child transforms into a butterfly herself. Lepidopteran abstraction notwithstanding, what this means in real life is a Saturday afternoon trip to a New Jersey mall.

Was there even a reason for going, a real reason like something we needed, or was it mindless entertainment, or better yet an Adventure Experience, Kali's term for car trips? We're going on an Adventure Experience! For all she knows "Adventure Experience" is a commonly used term. Knowing that your child is in the car seat strapped in, admiring the world as it passes, yelling *SLOW DOWN!!!* when you're driving no faster than sixty miles per hour, yelling *STOP!!!* when we're midway over the Ben Franklin Bridge in the center lane, knowing that this is no simple trip to the mall but an *Adventure Experience* intensifies everything, addles perception so we have an eye out for *adventure* the same way when walking along the paths of the nature preserve near the airport we have *eyes peeled* for caterpillars in the fall or tiny baby turtles in the spring. *The peeling of eyes* is something parents pass down to their children, and it's the most important activity, awareness sweeping the immediate environment for anything of interest. My eyes were certainly not peeled after trying and failing to write all morning and then driving over the bridge to New Jersey and then to the Cherry Hill Mall, negotiating winding traffic around the mall itself, obeying the signs, anticipating unpredictable movement from all surrounding automobiles. A car pulled out of a space and I waited for it before sliding into the spot where it was, like hermit crabs intent on consumption, something I remember and note now because Mamou in the passenger seat didn't think I gave the minivan exiting the space enough room to extract itself, which precipitated a spat of exasperation back and forth in the front seats and surely bright-eyed observation in the backseat although I didn't look in the rearview as I pulled the car into the space, too close to the car on the right side, Mamou said, precipitating another spat of exasperation back and forth until I reversed and resettled our car down the middle of the expanse of blacktop delineated by two white lines of paint. Parked, I held Kali high, cradled in my right arm, a light mist settling like miniature airborne eggs on uncontrolled wisps of her blondish-red hair.

We sat in a booth at an upscale chain restaurant that serves local, seasonal, low-calorie items and somehow seems to get every detail right. The décor, the dimmed but not dark lighting, the welcoming scent of grilled cedar planks (unusual when stepping out of a car onto a massive parking lot), the sounds leaning toward upbeat nostalgia for '90s indie like Belle & Sebastian, also once astounded to hear Vetiver's "More Of This" at low volume in the background, the pleasant service ("our menu is celebrating spring now so you'll see a lot of . . ."), and of course the perfectly palatable food including by far the best grilled chicken tenders kids' meal on the planet, with smoked mashed potatoes and a pile of firm, crispy green beans. All knives, salt and pepper shakers, and sugar packets were moved as far away from Kali as possible. Once she squirmed and tried to slide under the table, her mother produced her work phone with unlimited data and we anesthetized the child with streaming video. Kali watched animated Lego ninjas battle or brightly colored circular birds careen around as they communicated in the Esperanto of exaggerated gesture (the subtitles, for some reason on, only relayed emotion, like <<<anger>>>).

I recognized Molly Sullivan French, the Sixers' court-side reporter, as she entered holding a baby (maybe a year old) with her husband. Mamou and I, who have both lived in New York, were titillated by the presence of local celebrity. It's so rare to see someone recognizable when out on the streets or in an upscale mall chain restaurant. (Memorable NYC celebrity sightings for me included Liv Tyler, Jake Gyllenhaal, Willem Dafoe, Lenny Kravitz, David Byrne, Thurston Moore, George Plimpton, Anna Wintour, Donald Trump.) The first few times at this restaurant I ordered a beer even if it was early in the day. It seemed like the sort of place where a chilled glass of something hoppy and crisp would take the edge off everything before we ventured into the mall itself. I note the times I had once ordered a beer and considered it odd, like I had become a different person, more responsible, upstanding, new and improved, someone who would never order a beer at lunch at a restaurant at a mall with my child. My salad came, Kali's chicken tenders came, but Mamou's Thai steak salad lagged behind and when it did come it was just a regular old steak with a side of some sort of pilaf, which she didn't touch. We waved the server down to let her know that it seemed like the kitchen had mishandled the order, absolving the server of responsibility. I went to the bathroom, which is pristine and soothing, well-lighted, dark, with conscientious touches like grating under the urinal solving the challenge of the inevitable presence of piss stains on the floor. Everything seemed taken into consideration. The mirrors and lighting distorted my height and girth so I seemed taller and thinner (also could be the running and eating better and restricting alcohol intake) but they couldn't do anything to improve what I was wearing (jeans, black Sixers hoodie) or to straighten cowlicks standing at attention thanks to my removed winter hat. I resolved that next time we visited this upscale mall chain restaurant I would wear a blazer, a good clean collared shirt not made of flannel, and darker jeans, or maybe I'd wear the suit I wore on our wedding day, the one I'm supposed to wear when I take the train to DC and put everyone out of their misery.

After lunch Mamou walked to The Container Store, in a separate building along the outer ring of the parking lot, as I walked with Kali back to the car and then drove it to The Container Store and parked there, waiting for Mamou to pop out with a purchase to aid her constant organizational battle, most of which is caused not by ADHD or any will to disorganization but by a preponderance of plastic containers in the home dedicated to organizing her stuff. At this point I don't even attempt to intervene. It's a battle she has to fight for herself, one she'll never win until she discards all the stuff she thinks she needs to organize, which she'll never do because she's already purchased so many containers/organizers and wouldn't want all that plastic to go to waste. I can imagine some future if we fall on hard times in which her current low-level hoarder instincts unleash and we're buried in crap she purchases at box stores and thrift stores. In self-defense, I'll build a safe space for myself, an igloo of books. I'll live in there with my guitar, pedals, amp. For now, it seemed like she only needed one thing, a piece of plastic molded into compartments to store smaller pieces of plastic, and then we drove to another part of the multi-acre mall complex where there's a Guitar Center and an Aldi. There's also a huge discounted liquor store where once upon a darker time we would stop for cheap fancy beer for me and Muscato for her, back when Mamou was experimenting with an evening glass of wine for its soothing effects before she realized it made her face break out. On this day, however, we didn't enter the massive discount liquor store with its aisles of lower-priced bottles of beer from all over the world, a place that had once seemed like a sort of paradise, with a Sam Ash on one side, and beyond a Ruby Buffet (an Asian-run buffet specializing in crab legs), a Guitar Center.

Two giant musical instrument chain stores essentially separated by a giant liquor store: when we discovered this far-flung region of the Cherry Hill Mall, I thought *what could be better*? A little piece of strip mall heaven right here on Earth, completed by an Aldi where Mamou and Kali could shop for discounted non-namebrand victuals as I roam Guitar Center, where about a year ago I seriously looked at guitars and bought a cheap Vox modeling amp with a little tube in it, a small amp (20 watts, 8-inch speaker) that can sound something like an old Fender Tweed, a Fender Deluxe, various classic Vox amps of course, a Marshall, a Mesa Boogie, an Orange amp, maybe a few others, and lets you experiment with built-in effects like compression, chorus, overdrive, distortion, flanger, phaser, tremolo, delay, four types of reverb (spring, room, hall, plate), and tons of preset tones to invoke with the literal push of a button the ghost of Prince or Pink Floyd, on and on, but more so I got it for the headphone jack so I could play in the basement at night at a decent volume and only disturb the space between my ears. I already had a Fender Frontman 65R, a loud solid-state (not tube) amp with great clean tones and real spring reverb that nevertheless I realized as my ear became more sensitive, sounded a little like a tin can at times. With these two amps I used the twin outputs on a Boss DD-7 delay pedal and a setting to make the sound bounce back and forth between amps on either side of me, hitting a chord and letting it jump like a thought back and forth between neurons. But then of course one day last summer, as Mamou and Kali went on an Adventure Experience in the mall, I tried out tube amps at Guitar Center, thinking that it sometimes sounded like the space around the emitted sound seemed like the enclosure of a snow globe made from thick old glass from 1920s chemistry experiments, antique yet unbreakable beakers. I preferred of course for my playing to encase my basement lair in glass instead of something more like aluminum, same way I once preferred to drink fancy craft beer from a glass instead of a can.

The day of the Sunn O))) show, browsing the guitars, pedals, amps, I listened to a kid try the same amp I had played in the summer when I first really heard the glass-encasement sound. He was shredding, playing the same metal runs as half the guys (always guys) who try out a guitar or amp. All their approaches seem identical, the same runs learned from YouTube that originated maybe with Metallica or the guitarist for Whitesnake or some other hair metal band from mid-'80s MTV. I grew up exposed to that, always watched with fascination and disgust, never really liking it or buying any cassettes or wanting to learn to play that way. Now, thirty years later, here was this overweight white kid in an oversized sweatshirt, a baseball hat with a Swoosh on it, playing fast metal runs through a Fender Bassbreaker 15-watt combo amp, a new line from Fender with overdrive that makes it sound more like a Marshall. Which isn't quite like Coke trying to taste like Pepsi, or Nike trying to make a sneaker like Adidas, since the original Marshall amps were based on Fender amps, or something like that. The kid repeated the same metal leads, like Bach fugues gone bad, grimacing whenever he screwed up, saying he's playing so badly, like anyone cares, most likely not even the kid with him, a skinny anonymous white teenager in the throes of hormonal surge, acne, dark greasy curly hair pulled back in a little ponytail, the guitarist's gamer friend who's maybe considering learning drums but isn't interested in music as much as he's into first-person shooter games when out of his skull on sugar-encrusted gummy candy and energy drinks. I couldn't play the metal runs the kid plays, can't sit down with a Jackson or some other shredder axe instead of the Platonic ideal guitar forms from Fender or Gibson and then just let rip the way this kid does. There's something to that, I guess. If he heard me grab an MIM (Made in Mexico) Telecaster and plug-in to a sweet tube amp (for example, the Fender Limited Edition '65 Princeton Reverb 15W 1x12 combo amp with built-in tremolo and real spring reverb, neither typical black and gray nor tweed but "Bordeaux," an expensive amp I always try out and love before deciding that the Fender Blues Deluxe Reissue in tweed I bought last summer is just as good if ultimately too loud for my needs) and play an E minor chord and let it hang, savoring the sustain, and then run through slow bluesy selections from the pentatonic scale, my left wrist like hummingbird wings as I vibrate a note to make it come alive before playing some faster Garcia-inflected runs along the higher strings as I let the low E string fade, I'm sure the kid would be like quit playing like an old blues dude or some classic rock reptile like Neil Young. But I don't really care what he thinks, same as he doesn't care what I think, it's just this little performance where people who play alone in bedrooms come together under the guise of trying out new gear to play a bit for other people and out of the corner of their eyes note that someone seems to be standing there listening, maybe even watching your hands as you play something that sounds good thanks to the $1100 amp you want and the $800 Les Paul you're interested in but won't get because last year you bought a limited-edition American Stratocaster and love it to no end and don't want to get into a situation where you hardly play it because you're playing the Les Paul more often.

I justified the price of the Strat by saying I was acquiring a life partner. This would be the guitar I would have for life, forever and ever, the guitar I was waiting for all these years, the one that needed to come along at the right time, when my interest in playing met my ability to acquire it without taking on credit card debt, and so last spring, I allocated my annual bonus check to the provision of an electric guitar I couldn't stop looking at online. The bonus was nearly the same as the guitar's price, a guitar in a $200 case if purchased separately. Oiled ash body with the timelines in the wood defined like the striations on the coat of some gorgeous wild animal, nature's announcement to the world that the beast at hand is sleek and sinuous and not something to mess with or consider prey, or maybe more like the wavy lines in limestone along a canyon wall, some geologic calendar demarcating million-year eras of the past. A glossy maple neck, black pickguard, white pickups and knobs and the tip of the silver tremolo bar, a flat-out freaking beautiful guitar I acquired without playing first, assuming it would exceed my needs in function and form. If not, if over time I didn't love it, I'd be able to sell it for close to what I bought it for since it's a limited edition and in the very least an American-made Fender, considered more valuable than those made in Mexico or Japan (MIJ).

Somehow in the past seven years I've gone from a single man living in a small studio apartment with few possessions beyond books, music, clothes, and a computer, to owning a home with my wife where we raise our child. In the basement I have the guitar I'll have for the rest of my life, a more than suitable amplifier for now (although I do have my eyes on that Fender Princeton '68 reissue in "Bordeaux" with the 12-inch speaker), and a pedal board loaded with effects.

The pedal board is a palette of sound. In exchange for a one-time expense, as long as each pedal continues to function, the tubes of color never run out, at least that's how I justify the Echorec, Supa-Trem, and Holy Grail, each closer to $200 than the more typical

\$100 or the cheaper \$40 pedals. Once the board is established, once the spectrum of effects is complete, it can be tweaked and improved, but first all the colors are needed. The traditional order is distortion into overdrives into time-based effects like delays and reverb into soundwave modulation like phasers and tremolos into a looper, the sonic equivalent of red, orange, yellow, green, blue, indigo, violet. And once the guitar and amp are in place and the board is set, all that can be acquired is skill through play.

That's where I've been lately, music-wise, leaning against the southern wall of a reconstituted Spaghetti Warehouse, listening to the electronic music the band has chosen to play between the opener's set and their own, alone with my thoughts in a crowd of predominantly male backs facing the stage although there's nothing to see except the occasional roadie crossing in front of the amps with a semblance of discretion, stooping as though the lights aren't forty feet overhead, the way I duck when I enter or exit the subway and have sunglasses or reading glasses lifted to my forehead.

Lately I've been at the end of the rainbow, aware that the pot of gold can only be discovered via practice and play. It can't be acquired online from Amazon or Reverb in the form of a cheap Electro-Harmonix Soul Food overdrive modified by someone for an extra forty bucks so it sounds more or less like the mythical Klon Centaur overdrive available for between fifteen-hundred and thirty-five hundred dollars, although I suppose I could buy a Klon Centaur if I wanted to save for a year, do some freelance on the side, sell my most valuable pedals and rare/signed books, I could own one, but since I can't really hear the difference between an inexpensive clone and the actual Klon in comparison videos I'm fine with missing out on that experience. There's the Strymon Timeline or El Capistan, a multi-effect delay pedal or lauded tape-echo/reverb, that I wouldn't mind acquiring at one point, more reasonably priced, yet still expensive, something I could order from my phone well before Sunn O))) hits the stage, but I'm fine for now with the Echorec and DD-7 and Holy Grail pedals, the combined price of which is about the same as the Strymon Timeline, which requires about as much pedal board real estate as those three pedals too.

I've achieved what I wanted in the past years: I wanted to settle down, end the search, find someone who found me too, find someone willing to create a home with me and start a little family, and I wanted to find work that challenged me just enough to make it interesting but didn't take too much out of me or force me to work at night or on weekends or dress too nicely or even think much about what I do because I've mastered it and can perform its movements as though entering a tunnel from which I emerge at lunch and again when it's time to go home and intermittently of course throughout the day for water, coffee, meetings, bio breaks. I wanted to find a job that left me alone when I wasn't working, that paid well enough but not too much so I'd be worried about getting laid off to save costs, but also of course not too little so I felt exploited or disgruntled or spent half my time searching for better-paying jobs or had to take freelance work at night and weekends to make ends meet. I wanted to find a job that had good benefits, a casual dress code, and more than enough autonomy, a job I didn't have to drive to, one I could walk or bike or take the subway to, also a job that in some way seemed like it was on the positive side of the capitalist spectrum, a profitable business that helped others, and since I work on illustrated clinical books (called "atlases") with doctors, oncologists, radiologists, pathologists, cardiologists, endocrine gland surgeons, upper gastrointestinal and hepato-pancreato-biliary surgeons, thyroid surgeons, pediatric surgeons, surgeons breaking ground in the use of new technology, using robotics, since I spend most weekday hours working on these publications I'm contributing in some small way to the medical literature and therefore helping doctors and patients and their families more so than working on marketing campaigns for pharmaceutical companies or something along those lines. With fundamental earthly employment needs met, I focus on the spirit via consumption of guitar, amp, and pedals, construct my sonic palette, and immerse myself in tones, clicking switches on and off, tweaking knobs, until I find something that doesn't seem to require adjustment and lets me play without thinking about anything other than what I'm playing, not even thinking about that, the whole endeavor in my little area in the back of our basement like meditation.

The goal, if there even is one, is not to think about what I'm playing or adjusting notes. The goal, if it even exists, is just to play and record it on my phone and listen to it later that day if I'm playing in the morning before Kali wakes up or listen to it the next day if I play at night after she's gone to bed, listen to it and hear what I did, where I went, all the choices made while playing forgotten, all the adjustments made on the fly without really even thinking. At most I hear a pedal click now and then, or notice when a heavier effect comes on, distortion or a delay with the time knob cranked. It's self-hypnosis, and after ten or fifteen minutes, the next ten or fifteen minutes pass in a state of timelessness. Otherwise, in this timeless state achieved via three decades of guitar playing on and off (mostly acoustic from 1995 to 2015) and a year or two of re-immersion in electric guitar and acquiring pedals and amps, it seems now like I've achieved what I wanted to achieve and all that's really left to do is consume what I want and improve. The guitar in my hands and the pedals at my feet, the amp maybe not the final amp I'll own but an excellent one, albeit too loud for the little space I've created in the back of the basement, always worried when playing alone in the house (a rare phenomenon), that neighbors or the police are at the door and I can't hear them, so I keep the volume at a point where it's a full sound but not uncomfortable down there, always in part thinking I need a smaller amp, but then the perfect amp for my space costs more than a thousand dollars, which if I get and play for a decade or more, and absolutely love, is a fine price to pay, especially if I sell the Blues Deluxe to fund the upgrade, especially if getting the limited edition Fender '65 Princeton Reverb Reissue with the 12-inch Jensen speaker in a "Bordeaux" cabinet and wheat-colored grill, with the milky tube tremolo (that Fender has always called "vibrato" for some reason), especially if acquiring the amp I really want improves my playing, lets me sell off some pedals, and in the end saves my hearing, which after longer, louder sessions in the basement feels numbed, thudded, duller, if never to the point of ringing, then selling the Fender Blues Deluxe Reissue and acquiring the limited edition Fender '65 Princeton Reverb Reissue with the 12-inch Jensen speaker in a "Bordeaux" cabinet and wheat-colored grill seems like a wise purchase, an understandable one, a legitimate indulgence with long-term aesthetic and spiritual payoff therefore, right?

But the goal is to reach the spot *where I no longer want anything*, the way I don't imagine buying another electric guitar for years, maybe a Gibson Les Paul or a semi-hollowbody (Gibson 335) or a baritone electric or something very much unlike the Strat. At that point, when I have no more need for ideal objects and my needs are met work-wise I can continue buying books and music now and then, a new pedal maybe once a year, a good microphone for recording maybe, and continue to focus on the house, trying to learn how to fix basic things, follow interesting recipes every once in a while, help more with Kali's education, help make things easier for Mamou, help out in the neighborhood, start a band with ambitions to record and play shows, or just read more and more until that's really all I do, construct an online bookstore, sell used copies for a penny plus shipping, make friends with everyone at the post office, on and on and on.

The drums on the music they're playing between bands sound like guns, the snare hits sound like shots, and this perception makes me scout the exits again, envisioning scenarios in which the shooters enter through either of the two most possible entrances, but what if they enter through the back, break-in through the fence where the tour bus parks, slash throats backstage, take the stage in Sunn O))) gowns to applause and unleash machine gun fire on the crowd? In that case, in the far back right from the vantage of the stage, I'd probably not be hit. By the time I figured out what was happening, I'd be on the ground, doing my best reptilian shimmy along the bar floor in the back of the main room to the other bar in back and then to the exit.

Now they're playing Slint, who I saw with a musician friend from college maybe two years before, a guy I'll call The Eagle, who lives in Bethlehem, about an hour north of Philadelphia, a white American who plays in an otherwise all-Kenyan band and somehow has found himself working for a construction company, driving all over eastern Pennsylvania and western New Jersey, ordering materials and making sure they arrive at the job sites. He's rock solid physically and his hands are rough, his fingers thicker, he's gone gray and lost a lot of his long black hair from college, he has some sort of dermatological issue around his eye, and he's one of the better musicians I've played with in my life.

He got in touch because he had an extra ticket for Slint. We drank too much and smoked some weed and wound up at a bar near my place at closing time that was playing the evening news on a delay so I thought it was more like 11 o'clock although the show we saw hadn't ended until around then and then we'd been all over town drinking. I asked the bartender why they were shutting down so early, and he was like it's almost two in the morning. I was incredulous, not even believing my phone for a second, until I realized that the TV news had confused me. It's good the bar's closing, I laughed, because I should definitely be cut off.

I must have had coffee around six or seven and so was more energetic than I would normally be at that time of night, also accelerated to reunite with an old friend at a show, the nostalgia tour for Slint, who weren't much older than us, playing their classic albums *Tweez* and *Spiderland*, the cover of *Spiderland* a photo of the band members in water that looks like a quarry, the photo taken by Will Oldham, who The Eagle and I saw maybe a year after the Slint show at the same venue playing as Bonnie 'Prince' Billy with the Bitchin' Bajas. I can't remember if I had instruments in the basement after Slint or if The Eagle just slept on the couch.

Later I had amps and guitars and effects in the back of the basement and The Eagle and I played quietly late at night in the comfortable little space I've created in the back of our basement. He passed out with a guitar in his hands, something I hadn't seen since the '80s when it happened to the best musician I knew growing up, a virtuoso prodigy on violin and piano who had toured Europe in the American Boychoir School, added drums and bass guitar in high school, and then started playing electric guitar, as well as experimenting with cello and conducting, a total virtuoso on every instrument. He could pull on a strand of shag rug and pluck out "Old McDonald Had a Farm" and then improvise on the familiar melody when we were all lying around stoned.

That guy, my best friend from across the street growing up, developed a drinking problem early on. He'd wake up after a night of absolute vomitus teenage indulgence (I had a prescription for euphoria that called for three shots of bourbon followed by bong hits followed by three more shots of bourbon, maybe with a pint of water mixed in, that achieved euphoria for an hour or so before things went downhill), he'd wake from a night of way too much hard alcohol and when everyone else was throwing up with the morning sun or pledging they'd never drink again, he'd pour himself a high ball of scotch and down it. He developed a taste and a tolerance and a need for it in a way I had never seen before and haven't seen since. He eventually switched to jazz bass and drums, although of course he could still play violin, piano, and guitar unlike anything I'd seen. It was like he walked around and had a magic power in his pocket because he was, unlike everyone else walking around, a virtuoso on multiple instruments, but by his mid-twenties he found Alcoholics Anonymous and then God. His mother had perfect pitch and had been the minister of music at the local Presbyterian church. She composed music sitting in a chair in front of the television with a game of Solitaire laid out on the ottoman.

My friend's music lacked evil, the satanic edge, the rebelliousness, that nocturnal if not necessarily infernal orientation on the moral spectrum. His alignment was lawful good, essentially, like a paladin in Dungeons & Dragons, which he never had time or interest to play in elementary school because he had to practice piano and violin. He needed a touch of evil to give his music and playing and *sensibility* an edge, and maybe via drink, if he had ever learned to manage his drinking instead of completely restrict it, he could touch the hem of evil's Levi's. It was almost like he had a fatal flaw in his playing related to excessive whitebreadness, a natural resource and native instinct that led, naturally, to following in his mother's footsteps and becoming the minister of music at a progressive Unitarian-type church in one of the wealthiest towns north of New York City.

In an alternate reality, I was a little better on guitar, our friend Stone played bass, and Dave played drums and from an early age we had a great little band (**L**ee, **S**tone, & **D**ave) that took over the world, all of which never occurred in reality because we had preoccupations and personalities that kept that ideal alt-reality from occurring, or none of us had a sufficiently domineering personality to ensure the formation and evolution of a band like that, plus Stone never played bass, only strummed basic chords on an acoustic guitar or played barre chords up the neck on electric (an Ibanez, like Weir) when I took Garcia-inflected leads on a lovely Squire Telecaster (butterscotch body with white pickguard, maple neck, made in Korea, ultimately stolen during winter break of my junior year in college) as we played complete concerts of Dead covers in my bedroom after school. We smoked some weed either behind my house if no one was home or on the front porch behind the bushes or in my room, covering the bowl with a guitar pick and blowing the smoke into a towel rolled tight and tied off with rubber bands. The hit rag developed hundreds of amber and brown, lip-shaped stains on it. And then we played, not all that loud, recording it with headphones in the microphone jack of my stereo, and then we played the cassette back while dipping (Copenhagen for me, Kodiak for Stone), watching TV. After Stone left, it was time for dinner and then homework, listening to Jimi Hendrix's *Nine to the Universe* on vinyl, or Remmy Ongala's *Songs for the Poor Man* on CD, or a three-cassette Nusrat Fateh Ali Khan concert from Paris, often with the television on and the sound low, as I sat in a comfortable high-backed black chair with an ottoman and knocked out math and Spanish and science homework and then did my English and History reading and whatever else, before I grabbed my electric guitar and plucked unplugged, watching a sitcom or sports before I read in bed before sleep.

In Louisville around the same time the kids in Slint were playing what would become the foundations for Post-Rock in their basements or garages or practice spaces, united and way more talented than we were, turned on to more interesting contemporary music, harder music I've never really loved. The Eagle, also never into hardcore, was a devout of the Allman Brothers and ZZ Top and New Orleans blues guitarists before becoming an ethnomusicologist and studying in Kenya, writing a dissertation on Kenyan pop and often playing in bands with Kenyans. Like my across-the-street virtuoso friend growing up, The Eagle had studied piano when he was young but then switched to guitar. His talent seems more in his taste and particularity than virtuosity but also accuracy of recall and ability to replicate what he remembers and do so with some edge. That seems to be what's necessary, the way the night seemed threatening as I left the house when I realized I was alone on the street after dark on a weekend for the first time in a long time, mist rising from melting snow, the fog heavy and insidious.

Slint's *Spiderland* still on, I wonder how I'll get home after the show. Will I walk back to Broad Street and then take the subway south to my neighborhood? Will I grab a cab? Start walking down Tenth Street looking over my shoulder for an empty taxi? I've walked all the way to Market Street before finding one. Or I could walk all the way home, which I've done more than once, enjoying the journey on foot to our place on Ninth Street. With a sense of generalized menace afloat the choice has significance. One could lead to a traumatic event, a beatdown, although there's not much to mug me for other than my phone and nearly empty wallet.

Debit cards have probably reduced petty robbery more than any organized law enforcement effort. So often all I can say to a so-called panhandler is that I only have my ATM card. I'm not drinking so I have some cash in my pocket I'd be happy to hand over but as always I know I'm not the primary target, although as I age, as I stiffen and slow, as I seem out of place at night on certain streets or descending the piss-stink stairs to the subway, my quarry quotient increases. If I take a cab nothing will happen. I haven't spent a dime on beer so I can justify ten or twelve dollars to make it home ten minutes after the show lets out. But where's the Adventure Experience in that? Ears ringing, searching the driver's every utterance for significance, finding it of course in every word, summation of the night and state of the world.

I had Uber but then deleted it. Whenever the Broad Street Line subway wasn't running because someone had fallen or been flung to the tracks ahead of an oncoming train, the price would be inflated thanks to hundreds of other ride requests. I deleted the app after news broke of the initial Muslim ban when thousands spontaneously protested the outrageous executive order to halt immigration from seven Muslim countries where Trump didn't have business relations and the Taxi driver guild or union stopped taking passengers to and from JFK Airport. Uber saw an opportunity to cash in, or so it was understood, causing friends to post images of their deleted Uber app, which I then deleted too, although I didn't need much provocation since I rarely used it and didn't like having it on my phone. I didn't trust it, thought it was tracking me somehow, I had an intuitive paranoid response to the app, so if I could delete it as a political statement, all the better.

The subway is inexpensive but there's the uncertainty of how long I'd have to wait for a train, standing on the platform, looking at my phone, a sparse group of concertgoers nearby, a sense that we've wandered onto the savannah's tall grass. Walking home is the slowest, cheapest, most direct option involving varied scenery, open air, and some Adventure Experience potential, so there's no decision to be made, although it's clear that the decision to walk home relates to being a tall male still more or less in the prime of life, with improving health, wearing a winter hat that adds three inches to my 6'3" frame.

When I first moved to Philadelphia more than ten years ago the newspapers were calling the city Killadelphia. Hundreds were shot each year, mostly young black men in drug-related battles in peripheral neighborhoods. The streets were empty at night. Except for a few pedestrian thoroughfares, no one was on the streets, so if you were walking home from a show or a bar or a date late it'd just be an empty block ahead, nearly silent beyond the distant city hum, and if someone were coming blocks ahead, the prudent thing to do would be to cross the street well in advance. I'd often see people cross to the other side of the street as I advanced toward them, as though I were the adversary, the potential mugger, the senseless murderer. I liked thinking that someone found my presence up ahead intimidating enough to cross the street or maybe more so the approaching pedestrian only wanted to avoid the inevitable awkwardness of nodding hello or more likely acknowledging another's existence by respectfully ignoring that existence.

A woman exists near me. Her pants are made of a type of synthetic fabric that wiggles when one walks, like a delicate petunia in the breeze, like Jello during a minor earthquake (2.0 on the Richter scale). The pants are loose along most of the legs and flare at the thigh in an old-timey militaristic way, but not around the lower curves of her posterior. I Google "thigh flared riding pants" and discover that she's wearing a contemporarily upgraded jodhpur, which originated in India centuries ago, became popular in the West through the sport of polo, and were part of the uniform for the Women's Land Army during World War II. They definitely have a sporty militaristic equestrian vibe to them. Jodhpurs. Huh. I turn toward the bar and note a man seated at a table behind me on a bar stool-type chair, slouched in his seat, arms folded like a connoisseur assessing some delicacy when really he's just mesmerized by the nearby combination of gluteal muscle and fat accentuated by jodhpurs, and he nods at me, like yeah, check that out, which disturbs me and turns my sight around in an instant, as though the imagined terrorists just appeared on stage for real.

It's fine for me to eat half a cookie and a lollipop and come alone to a Saturday night Sunn O))) concert since I'm one-hundred percent impervious to lechery. A tall white male, at this point somehow indisputably middle-aged, bearded, head addled with orally consumed tetrahydrocannabinol, no one really makes me feel uncomfortable, no one in the area imagines what it might be like to bend me over and take me from behind or otherwise. At almost every turn, everywhere I choose to stand, I am not caressed by desirous eyes, hypothetically fondled by men who need to actively look away from the attractant in the woman's derrière, responding to an ancient mating cue biologically embedded in them by nature, controlled by it as though the universe manipulated the dials on their desire to ensure propagation of the species. Now I have to think about this guy behind me all night, the woman to my right in the ecstatic-assed jodhpurs, the triangle we compose, its angles electrified by the intensity of the guy behind me staring at the woman in the jodhpurs, the intensity of the presence of the woman in the jodhpurs in general, the intensity with which I focus on the limited action on the stage, this unintentional process-based performance art involving roadies setting up as endless clouds of dry ice flow in thicker emissions over the wall of massive speaker cabinets. More so, I have to *not* think about this Bermuda Triangle of attractant, amorousness, and avoidance. Instead, how about the basketball game tomorrow? I'll wait to buy a cheap ticket when demand drops on Stub Hub, maybe an hour before the game, not really caring where I sit, just wanting to pay less than $30 and see the Sixers beat the Celtics, won't drink or buy food.

All the Craigslist ads for amp and effect pedals and the twelve-string guitar I posted this morning, all the digital scheming, selling shit, buying shit, browsing shit, sifting through responses from obvious scammers who want me to ship the twelve-string guitar to California or India in exchange for a cashier's check or money order, and in return I say sure I'll take care of it right away once you provide your social security number, mother's maiden name, links to all checking and savings accounts, and while you're at it how about you save me the trouble and just send me the passwords too? At times when I look at a guitar, even though I'm not interested in acquiring another, I suspect that it's been adjusted to seem upscale. It's the cheapest Fender Squier with a serial number on the back of the headstock added that begins with the letter M, indicating that it's a Mexican Fender and therefore worth more, or it starts with US to indicate an American Fender worth a thousand dollars or more. I can't spot the differences that might require you to remove the neck and pickguard and root around inside, so whenever I consider a guitar, unless it's a cheap version already, I say never buy a guitar on Craigslist for more than $300. But scrolling through the constantly updating feed of electric and acoustic guitars, bass guitars, keyboards, cymbals and complete drum kits, cords, amps of all types, microphones, mixers, monitors, effect pedals, synths, scrolling through and occasionally adding to the electronic bazaar has replaced social media for me in a conscious effort to *keep to myself for a while*, to miss out on everything, take solace in ignorance, find joy in avoidance of friends' accomplishments, all new baby pics, all new vacation pics, all new professional achievements, all new birthdays, all new indignation at political horror show.

In my childhood bedroom I remember the first little white plastic record player I had, playing Kiss records as I went to sleep, something my mother didn't think was a good idea but my father didn't worry about it. There's nothing wrong with loving music and everything it suggests. The otherworldly phenomenon of the needle tracking across the grooves at a set speed produces amplified vibrations))), you see beyond the sound you hear, like every song were real, had three-dimensional shape, described experiences that occurred in physical form like anything on TV, and it could be played over and over, unlike television at the time, the reception through the antennae atop the roof not always producing a clear image, another impressive variety of magic for five, six, seven year olds. Not until I was eight did I have a turntable and a pair of speakers that closed like a suitcase and could be carried away for mobile use, although it never moved from where it was on the floor in my bedroom, sometimes with the rectangular Magnavox cassette recorder, an elegant tripartite construction of speaker, tape player, and squarish silver buttons, that I placed next to the speakers to record whatever record I had borrowed from a neighborhood friend. I watched the needle track across the record as the cassette wound from the left spool to the right spool, taking it all in, like I was stealing it, getting a discounted version for private portable personal use, creating a little collection of pirated audio material. Aerosmith's *Live Bootleg* album was the first record I taped this way. We walked around the neighborhood with the cassette player in hand, blasting "Mama Kin" best it could. Now we would download songs from Spotify and carry around a cheap Bluetooth speaker in a backpack.

Kali on her potty in the morning, calling for her tablet, insisting on watching Spotify, not the educational apps from PBS or Starfall. Netflix she calls Spotify but there's really no need to correct her since by the time she knows the difference they'll both be supplanted by something else. The dominant music transmission vehicle in my lifetime has advanced or at least mutated so far from vinyl to cassette to compact disc to mp3 to stream. At the Princeton Record Exchange the past few years, the prices have jumped in the vinyl bins. Simple horizontal lines about a centimeter long have invaded en masse and jacked the price of $1.99 records to $7.99. The bargains, the finds, the hotspot in the store is now the wall with used CDs and even more so the bins with random discs, most under $3.99. With everything available on Spotify and YouTube, the in-person search of bins for physical objects to take home, for example something listened to and liked online, becomes more significant, nostalgic, atavistic, although it wouldn't hurt if the store had a GPS-driven search engine, an app to search the store's complete catalogue and receive directions to the target object like you're driving somewhere.

It seems like we're getting somewhere now, someone's on stage performing the ceremonial mic check. *What if it's them* I think and then note to my phone. I heard drums, so it's a recording, not live, unless drummers are hidden behind the wall of amps. If asked to stop texting or tweeting or whatever I'm doing, flashing open my phone every few minutes, alighting torso and face and fingers in heavenly smartphone glow, I'll say I'm writing an article. That'll be my alibi. I note that *writing an article will be my alibi*, but "alibi" autocorrects to "Albion," befitting a crowd primarily descended from European stock, the traditional hard-rock historical focal point of ancient Britannia, the Middle Ages, dreary castles, peasant villages set aflame by marauding hordes, wizards and wenches, lutes and folkloric lyricism, every nose with its wart. The atmosphere, here, now, seems transportive thanks to green and blue lights streaming through dry ice, as though they dye the air. A jump cut back to the days when this room housed the dining room of a Spaghetti Warehouse, a split second showing its first post-industrial past, and now this moment, the

Angel of Death in green and blue, a velvety turquoise suffusion all around.

It would be easier not to take notes, turn off mind/relax/float downstream, submit to the temptation to return to apathy, where I may have been, not apathetic about work, family, aspirations, entertainments, but more so unreflective, not thinking, unaware of my thoughts as they occurred, thinking without registering a thought's appearance. Thoughts now come fast and assert themselves, as though aware that some are being noted for later inclusion in a compilation of thoughts, a thought-preservation project. Here's their shot to not just flit across consciousness but to display themselves in splendor, strut for a moment, recorded for later use, misspelled in quasi-literate shorthand I surreptitiously thumb to my phone, one part consideration, trying to minimize light pollution, another part espionage, a fantasy unfurled from last night (the Disney movie, the frozen chicken tenders in the shape of dinosaurs fed to our child, some of which I snacked on) and the trip to the Cherry Hill mall, an Adventure Experience into the heart of common-denominator capitalist lameness. A Twitter novel of just the gist formatted like these notes, misspelled shorthand, the heart of the matter reduced to essential sinew. It's a minimalist band, after all. Visibility, the way airlines refer to it, reduced. The balcony obscured by clouds, dusty rose now instead of turquoise. The balcony above me, the wall to my left, unseen humans to my right, the stage ahead at a slight angle through the fog.

I've laid off Instagram lately too. I've only taken images of the child I post every few weeks if her spirit's been adequately captured. A mutual appreciation society of other people's kids won't make America great again. It gets tiring, feeling obliged to drop one's thumb on the outline of a heart several times a day. It adds to the sense of the wheel turning too quickly, cranked ahead by minor duties throughout the day, all the micro responsibilities, small tasks and repetitive movements. Everything reduced, when taken together, amounts to too much.

I want to write something with a Mixolydian progression, I note, not exactly sure what I mean. I think I mean something braided. A series of flags made of chainmail. Modal, metallic phrases in perpetual undulation.

The show starts, dropped-tuned (conventional E tuning dropped to C, maybe even B) distorted guitars drone, the "singer" in robes seems from my vantage to wear a grotesque mask and a formless gown of some sort. A hairshirt? It's hard to tell from the back of the venue, off to the side, leaning on the soundproofed wall, through a thick scrim of dry ice, the former Spaghetti Warehouse transformed thanks to blue cathedral illumination, the solid cloud bank in the room working with the lights to lend solidity and color to the tone. The singer himself speaks in something that sounds like Romanian, Bulgarian, a southeastern European language inflected with Latin, an introductory lecture on the nature of the beast, the persistence of the Middle Ages, the Dark Ages, the Medieval stumble through dusk and night before the dawn of the Renaissance and rationality. Darkness persists, belief in ghosts, magic, binary spirits seeking influence, their forces in constant struggle in the air above us and inside us, masquerading these days as scientifically identified neurochemical and neuropsychological processes controlling our impulses, unconscious desires controlled with active reminders to pay attention to what we're doing so not to otherwise succumb to white and black spirits all around seeking possession.

The singer who doesn't sing, the front man, the focal point of the stage with the musicians draped in robes no more than silhouettes, seems like a Jawa doing Kabuki. Jawas appear early in *Star Wars*, the first installment from 1977. They have the droids, they wear brown robes with hoods, they're scavengers. It's like a slow shadow-play, a recital of protozoan humanity, old country ooze, reanimated for our entertainment. I imagine if terrorists enter, the singer will spin them in a web of lights and fog.

His arms are out like a bad kid in my neighborhood when I was growing up who one gray and humid afternoon rode his bike no-handed, fists in the air, mouthing the opening of Black Sabbath's "Iron Man," an image burned into my memory, although now the bad kid's bike seems more like a squadron of amplified Harleys.

Teeth-rattling bass. My teeth, upper left side, literally rattle. There's a thread of pain through the gum somehow squelched by turning my head and sucking the offending area with my tongue. What if they've cracked something? My incisors once were longer and sharper, pointier. Without my consent, the orthodontist shaved my vampire fangs to societally acceptable canines. As a child I read every vampire book available at the local library and placed the scariest volumes at the bottom of the pile, as though the illustrations squirmed with life, the undead presence in my bedroom neutralized by a pillar of books atop it. I wonder if I can sue Sunn O))) for dental costs required as a consequence of their sub-bass? I wonder if discomfort in my upper-left fang indicates that I'm officially too old to venture out to shows like this? At the Swans show last year, standing in the same spot against the wall in the back by the bar, I palmed the wall and felt it vibrate, aware that the loose denim fabric around my knee trembled. The volume must affect everyone's skin and thoughts. The watery surface of our eyes must ripple.

The intimidating bad kid in my neighborhood who one afternoon long ago rode his bike with fists in the air acting out the opening of "Iron Man" died young thanks to alcoholism. He lived at home most of his life and littered fifths of cheap vodka in the honeysuckle bushes along the path between our neighborhood and the old village streets. He embodied "Iron Man" in a way he never recovered from, or he was able to convey the spirit of cartoonish evil because as a teenager he was already a Wicker Man aflame inside. Sabbath offered the illusion that straw on fire was heavy metal. Mouthing the lyrics ("heavy boots of lead, I hear voices in my head") transformed him into Frankenstein's robot, indestructible, invincible. Music supported him, transformed him, gathered forces and stood at attention behind him. I saw it and believed it.

The lights are now purple and green, like at the end of *Kung Fu Panda 3* when Po transforms into the Dragon Warrior, fully realized, thanks to everyone sending their chi to him. It's like the end of a sports movie when the overmatched protagonist, against all odds, overcomes every obstacle, every physical and psychological and societal limitation, and wins, the sort of movie that makes manly men weep. Complete self-realization. Best self elevated. Transcendent. God-like. Psychedelically omnipotent. Synchronized with the universe.

Longing for supernatural power appeals to children who hear "no" a thousand times a day, are all desire all the time and are always thwarted by parents whose energy the child depletes to the point of only being able to start an installment of the *Kung Fu Panda* animated series and watch it with the happy and totally engaged child for the umpteenth time.

The last time I met a friend for happy hour, something we used to do with regularity, almost every Friday afternoon, and now limit to once every few months, I explained the extraordinary power of the *Kung Fu Panda* series. It was extraordinary, really, this *Kung Fu Panda* trilogy, capped by its third and greatest installment, the triumphant concluding payoff as good as *Rocky* or something along those lines, the characterization, the storylines, the animation, the music, the humor, the wisdom, all the product of hundreds of humans working together to pull it off. It made me weepy, a little bit, not being part of something like that. It made me want to submit to Los Angeles traffic to work with a team of writers to sculpt an extraordinary script, so well done, so enjoyable by parents and children without ever seeming schlocky.

My friend responded can you imagine what a previous iteration of you seven or eight years ago would've said about your *Kung Fu Panda* admiration?

I said my previous iteration hadn't seen *Kung Fu Panda* so I'm sure he would've said he would need to see it based on my future iteration's rave review.

I really do mean what I say about *Kung Fu Panda*. I need something to believe in and so, for now, I believe in *Kung Fu Panda*. I also have temporary privileged insider status in this world of animated entertainment geared toward children and parents at once. *Paw Patrol*, *Wild Kratts*, *Shimmer and Shine*, *Ninjago*, on and on. I know all the shows. *Inside Out*, *Zootopia*, *Frozen*, *Penguins of Madagascar*, *Bee Movie*, *Despicable Me* and the *Minions* movies, the *Lego* movies (*Lego Batman*, particularly), I've memorized them. Bergman, Herzog, Tarkovsky, Godard, Kurosawa, Ozu, my collection of Criterion Collection DVDs collect dust for now. *Kung Fu Panda* makes it OK, for a while, in part as visualization of ecstatic assumption and fulfillment of personal powers when fully engaged with the community, not to mention, again, the end of *Kung Fu Panda 3* when Po hovers in air in "the spirit realm" upon a translucent dragon of fire, a representation of a soul manifest and absolutely optimized, which I associate at this point with the sound of my guitar when I look down at the pedals that are on and their current settings and think oh man I should stop now and take a photo so it always sounds like this, or when all the hundred million movements of the day assume a rhythm and make sense and don't wear me out or frustrate, or when the hours pass at work when deeply engaged. Sometimes someone assumes this state in public, usually an athlete who enters the so-called flow and becomes unstoppable. Natural talent and ceaseless twice-daily practice and training sessions align to dominate their opponents, effortlessly, thoughtlessly, as though they've achieved another level of play.

Today, in New York, Aodhán Ó Riordáin, an Irish politician leads a rally against Trump. The Gaelic-named man gained exposure for ripping Trump in Irish parliament in a perfectly phrased, impassioned speech that was filmed and went viral. At the time, he, like the panda Po, seemed to possess and arrange his powers and transmit them as though lasers emanated from his brain in direct transmission to millions of viewers intent on resistance, hungry birds with mouths wide open for food from a source of respectable morality and rationality. His speech seemed like a proclamation from on high, and although he was a middle-aged Irish guy in a suit with a conventional emerald trill, his voice sounded supercharged with urgency and import. All his experiences and learning combined to meet the moment, the waves of history he rode. Somewhere in New York, less than a hundred miles up a three-lane road, he leads a rally as we stand here exposed to thick heavy sound and thick colored air.

In an audience instead of on a stage or the spirit world, I am not feeling all that self-actualized or realized or optimized but right now at least I can accept who I am. It's not like Sunn O))) aspires to become Bruno Mars, who I've heard of but have never heard, or have their music licensed for soft-drink advertisements. Imagine sustained distorted sub-bass in a thirty-second film of a pick-up truck conquering the western tundra. Or sustained distorted sub-bass in advertisements for mass-produced cheeseburgers. Or sustained distorted sub-bass in automobile insurance advertisements (other than the unpredictable ones for Geico). Or sustained distorted sub-bass in advertisements for pharmacological interventions for erectile dysfunction. It's not like the primary Sunn O))) musicians Stephen O'Malley and Greg Anderson, or Hungarian vocalist Attila Csihar, want Sunn O))) to become something more than it is. I'm sure they want reasonable evolution, changes in instrumentation or effects, various collaborations like the one with Scott Walker, mid-'60s leader of The Walker Brothers, a band of heart-throbs nearly as popular as The Beatles at one point, who gave up fame and fortune for unconventional, idiosyncratic art music. After a certain point, there's no return for the band, they're on a trajectory followed by an audience, and everyone's interested to see where it goes.

Most in the audience don't have such a following, although I suppose anyone's self-consciousness, self-awareness, and memory amount to an audience of sorts, knowledgeable fans of the self who were *there* for the early years and can track the passage of time via our movement through it, the way a flag reveals the wind. A long-term relationship with an entity that relies on you to exist but has no knowledge of the particularities of your existence almost amounts to something spiritual. I'm thinking of the history of the country you live in, the history of your favorite teams, the history of your favorite bands, unlike for example the history of friends and family.

I should quote Proust, the patron saint of memory, but instead will talk about Sirius radio, how my old car died last summer and we replaced it with a safe and reliable Subaru that came with satellite radio trial offer for a month. Sirius, it turns out, offers a station devoted to a band I listened to almost exclusively in the late '80s, my final high school years, before in college and afterwards in the '90s and '00s and the teens of the twenty-first century I moved away from them to discover everything I had missed during those pivotal years, only now and then playing a cassette and then mp3s of a concert from Veneta, Oregon in 1972, about six months after my birth, now and then awed by their extended improvisational sections, the interplay of the guitars (the rhythm guitarist more or less like a horn section; the lead guitarist exactly like a former bluegrass banjo player equally immersed in acid and Coltrane's sheets of sound) and the new keyboardist's piano and the drums and bass (as distinctive as the lead guitarist, always seeming like he's wandering, artfully avoiding expected tonic notes, until he drops a monumental chord to resolve it all at just the right moment). It had been something I'd been so into that I had to put it down since it was too much its own thing, not just the protein on the plate but the source of all sustenance (breakfast, lunch, dinner, snacks, and intoxicants). Now, more than fifty years since the band started, they have their own satellite radio station on which recordings of at least two complete live concerts are played each day.

A few months into my first year out of college, I was working at a restaurant when someone said I had a call (five years or so before the proliferation of cellphones). It was my roommate. He said he had some bad news. I should sit down for it.

Jerry died.

What? Seriously? I thought a friend from college or maybe even one of my parents had died, or our apartment had burned down, but it was only the death of someone generally beloved but distant. At the time I was trying to make space for new music. Those foundational experiences driving to and from shows in Buffalo, Indiana, California, DC, the psychedelic experiences too, listening to the New Year's 1987-88 broadcast when Dave's parents were away, traveling down through the shifting, symmetrical depths of an Oriental rug, seeing the first Led Zeppelin album cover in color and thinking it was just a special edition Dave's brother owned, all the kaleidoscopic bacchanalian dance parties with seventy-thousand revelers focused on one sight and sound, returning home from Giants Stadium and hearing straight-up classical music in the hum of the overhead bathroom fan as orange flowers on the wallpaper turned graceful pirouettes and all that knowledge of set lists, lyrics, chords, trivia, the shoebox filled with all those Maxell and Memorex cassettes, was in quarantine. It was the music of innocence, in a way, and in college and soon after I wanted the music of experience, music made by people more or less my own age, and I wanted the music I was making too. I never conceived of something like Sunn O))) at the time, even if during my senior year in college I had heard the drone on an early Earth album nearly wreck someone's stereo speaker.

By the end of college I had moved away from playing electric guitar. I was mostly playing acoustic although I owned and occasionally played an unplugged Gibson 335 semi-hollowbody copy, a Sebring I never really loved that replaced the wonderful Squier Telecaster stolen over winter break my junior year in college. That first year after college I played acoustic in a sort of circular rhythmic strumming pattern as I bounced fingertips on and off the strings, a technique that somehow sometimes created an effect like three separate sounds at once, a technique I was excited about when I heard it on tape but that when I played at open mics around Austin didn't really make anyone excited. It may have made some people excited if I'd kept at it and refined it or if I saved and bought an amp and eventually a car and played loud electric music in that style with like-minded musicians but the keyword of the time was *restlessness*.

A year of life after college was so significant. Every day working, every night roaming the city on my bike in search of music, drinks, parties, hookups, love, experience, something to write songs about, new friends I'd form the band with that was always meant to sweep me up in its destiny. I was willing and swayable by fate, intentionally rudderless if the current seemed like it'd sweep me out into a sea of excitement, but it ultimately sent me away from music, into Central America, solo travel, journal writing, writing stories, describing what I saw and thought. If I'm really honest about my early experience after college trying to play music, not even a year of it, it's like I first encountered basic obstacles, and their existence, including setbacks and criticisms, seemed to me wholly significant, so much so that I opted for sitting by myself, reading, writing, realizing how much there was to read, aware that the lyrics I wrote for songs with two chords were expanding until there was no way I'd remember them all, too many verses, like the text in the cartoon dialogue bubble overwhelming the image, spilling out of its frame. Words gained importance as music frustrated me. There were only so many takes I could record of my songs. It never occurred to me to cut the lyrics down to Old Country growls and sermons in faux-Latin and reduce the two chords to a single droned and extremely distorted note.

It seems like we're all standing for an endless national anthem. But I'm not sure what the country is. One without borders, its citizens whoever would stand through a Saturday night of entertainment like this. To call this "entertainment" is pushing it. This is more like Dungeons & Dragons music, something that should stream from every *Monster Manual* and *Player's Handbook* like those Christmas cards that emit tinny versions of "Silent Night."

I think *this is like D&D music* and immediately see a grid of graph paper, thin blue lines across the white sheet, the paper used to diagram homemade modules, the term for the pre-fabbed campaigns and floor plans from Gary Gygax and friends. Without searching, how much can I remember of the game, other than the multi-sided dice and the names of monsters, all of which I've always remembered pretty well, all the way from the lowly orcs and bugbears to chromatic dragons and Demogorgon and Asmodeus, essentially Satan himself. I don't worry about the time I spent playing D&D in third grade, the drawings of dragons on piles of gold pieces (easy to draw), the subsequent interest in mythology that led to an interest in literature, extended metaphor, allegory, although nothing as clear as the myth of Persephone and the pomegranate (she ate six seeds or half of it and had to stay in Hades half the year, which is why her mother Ceres mourns for half the year, giving us autumn and winter). Allegory that didn't resolve so easily I ultimately loved as a teenager. Kafka segued perfectly from mythology, as did lyrics to songs by Hendrix ("1983: A Merman I Shall Turn to Be" and/or "Voodoo Chile"), The Doors, Led Zeppelin, but really from the very beginning we're receiving mythology through children's books, all of them ending not happily ever after but with the protagonist falling peacefully asleep.

Kali freaked out watching TV when a dragon seemed to fall to its death in a movie. She had a stuffed animal in the form of a dragon she held onto and then she threw it down the stairs as though to mourn the death she saw in the movie, replicating it, crying, completely freaking out, refusing to receive consolation from her parents that the dragon didn't die, that it's a movie, and that her stuffed animal comes alive with her imagination. It's so rare for her to freak out over something like that. Julia Roberts was crying in a movie and Kali started crying in sympathy and wanted to make Julia Roberts feel better. Something like that is more common than freaking out over something she sees in a movie. Thunderstorms, loud motorcycles, and jackhammers scare her, but otherwise she's fearless, courageous, not apt to have her tantrum switch flicked.

I switched from music to writing in an instant. I was writing lyrics and poems and handwritten journal scrawls (indecipherable) but focused on writing songs to play on acoustic guitar, not simple strummer sing-a-longs. It was almost like something broke. I met the first round of obstacles on what could've been a heroic journey to some sort of minor success as a musician, and instead more or less stopped playing music and started writing stories and reading more. It was like pressure had built up of trying to play music without an amplifier (sold it to fly to Austin) or a car to drive the amp I didn't have to practice spaces to play with musicians I didn't know, and whenever I did manage to play with someone the styles clashed.

Everyone at college knew how to improvise, make music up on the spot, even friends who didn't regularly play an instrument strapped on an electric guitar or sat at the drum kit and made interesting rhythmic noise, but then after college I played with a drummer from the restaurant who was a good punk drummer but couldn't really do too much except play straight-ahead beats. Or I played with a guy who played alto sax but didn't know how to do anything other than hold a few notes and that sounded perfectly good but we weren't going to play together too often. He said I was the best guitarist he had ever played with, not saying much for me or the musicians he had played with, in part because *I used all the strings*. I didn't stick with it, endure it, let the clouds gather and break and then clear and gather and clear again and again.

My roommate, at a show for a local funk band that had a nice following, questioned whether I could stand on stage as master of ceremonies and also one time said that while my acoustic playing sounded cool it wasn't technically difficult so no one really into the technical aspects of guitar playing would be all that into it, and that opened a door in my head to a friend from college who said *I didn't have it* after I tried to sit in with him and another friend (who would later become a famous comedic actor) as they played bluegrass on mandolin and guitar. It was my first time trying to play bluegrass and I had never really listened to bluegrass so I just faked the style but I took the critique to mean *I didn't have it* generally as a guitar player, which maybe was true. I remember asking The Eagle in college if he could play what he heard in his head and he said he wasn't sure. I said I think maybe I could sometimes or was getting there. He said something like *well I guess you're not hearing much* or something like that, an uncharacteristic confidence killer from The Eagle. Of course every positive comment after sets at parties or around campus from people I hardly knew or requests for lessons from younger women and the guys standing up front watching my hands meant nothing. Enthusiastic comments from total strangers after I played open mics in Austin meant nothing. The handful of negative comments that stuck with me meant everything since they confirmed my doubts, something I hadn't encountered yet to a significant degree. In sports, doubts are confirmed by the final score, by the team's record at the end of the season, by statistics. But this was my first unquantifiable experience out of college. The dragon that had always sat on a pile of imaginary gold pieces inevitably flailed now that it was for real. My response wasn't to practice every day and night for hours and write better songs and hone what I was doing until the dragon took flight. Instead I rode my bike around and used tip money on pints of beer and saw bands (shows were free at first and then $2 at Emo's), trying to meet people to play with, hoping to meet women, and instead of doing either for the most part I started writing poems. Alone out at night, drinking beer, I'd write a silly surreal rhyming poem for an alluring woman and then I'd fold it into a paper airplane and throw it toward her table as I left the bar and headed to a show. The novelty and excitement of this led to writing stories. On a weekday off from restaurant kitchen work, I sat in a park near my apartment and wrote the beginning and middle of a story and then finished it later at a bar on a warm misty day in February. The story involved a band taking the stage and opening fire on the audience. I handwrote it and it felt cathartic, not only to write a story for the first time since my sophomore year in college but to seep frustrations out of the pen that had developed since moving to Austin the previous August. It had felt like forever of course, all that time, when it hadn't even been a year, no more than six months, but there was no patience. I wanted everything immediately. Our apartment couldn't confine me. I swept the ceiling with my fingertips. Paced like a caged beast before I jumped on my bike and rode around just to have more space and possibility, before finally lighting out for the territories, four months of solo travel on buses through Mexico and Central America, writing all the time.

The stage is bathed in purple fog, the front man from my vantage looks like the hero of an opera delivering an impassioned soliloquy reduced to groans and growls. He looks like an ogre elevated by expressions of human suffering. The sound keeps us all upright as it wears us down and we want to collapse.

Someone has farted oh so terribly. The gas someone has passed is oh so terrible. Everyone in my vicinity covers nose and mouth. My vetiver-reinforced ramparts are stormed, overwhelmed, absolutely vanquished. I can smell it through my eyes, ears, skin. I must be a suspect. Unable to stand still throughout the show, wavering, bopping, shifting weight, pulling out his phone every five seconds to text prayers to a higher power about his critical urge to poo. The new administration recently appointed as the head of the Environmental Protection Agency someone who had campaigned on a platform that included dismantling the Environmental Protection Agency. The virulent flatulence, oh so terrible, an omen of imminent devastation. The rivers on either side of the city, on either side of Philadelphia but also on either side of Manhattan, no longer reek. Runners and bikers along urban river paths exercise in places once off limit due to toxicity and stench. Eagles, hawks, osprey, so many raptors have made a comeback thanks to restrictions against DDT use.

The singer raises his fist and a few in the crowd do too. More raise their fists. One of the guys in front of me, the one who had told his friend he was so well read, raises his fist. Are they called "resist fists"? The fists of the black Olympic sprinters in Mexico City '68. I search for "black runners with raised fists." A protest for human rights, not Black Power, says Wikipedia.

Whatever's happening in the room is the undeniable climax of the show. There's something half-fascist, half-leftist about it. Resist fists in the air, a demonstration against the new administration, sure, but it also seems like some of those with raised fists are brainwashed. Some also raise devil horns (index and pinky fingers up with middle and ring fingers down, a gesture popularized by Ronnie James Dio, Ozzy's replacement in Sabbath, to ward off the devil), and some raise phones with the flashlight app engaged, or maybe some have an app that shows a Zippo lighter you can flip open and raise at concerts. Purple, blue, with black smoke, suggesting arrival at the end of the color spectrum (ROYGBIV). At first only the singer raised his fist and then it infected others and then it spread but I resist the impulse to raise a fist even if I understand it not as being brainwashed by an hour of droning detuned distorted guitars through a wall of Sunn amplifiers, not as a manly version of saying "uncle," I've had enough, I'm tired of standing in the slowly evolving colored fog listening to the sound of plate tectonics, of the leisurely settling of industrial pollution on medieval cathedrals, of the aging and weakening of everyone's bones, of inevitable cognitive and bodily decline, of time itself passing in a not entirely peaceful way, destroying everything in its path in the end, like slow-flowing lava. I resist the impulse to raise a fist in unison with the singer and maybe forty percent of the crowd not because I see it as a symbol of unity against the forces of oppression at hand, the incursion against civil liberties that somehow won the most powerful position in the world.

I resist the impulse to raise a fist in a show of resistance because I'm an observer. I don't want to go along with everyone else. Whenever I feel the urge to join a mass of people I try to maintain my space, except in sporting events where I release my spirit and share the joys and agonies along with the twenty thousand or more in the arena, and I simply feel good about it. At some concerts I've released myself into the audience, part of the whole, dissolved in a way that simply feels good and probably releases oxytocin in the brain. I want to resist the new administration but I don't want to do so by dropping my thumb on a heart shape or liking or retweeting or raising my fist or affixing a bumper sticker to my car. I don't want symbolic and ephemeral resistance. Donating to the ACLU and Planned Parenthood I suppose helps, and I've done that, but more so I want to put on my wedding suit et cetera and travel to DC, or better yet resist through writing, write an account of this night as a form of resistance, not sure how it is or if it is but it feels like it could be, as though it all somehow is: the aesthetic independence and obvious anti-capitalist approach of the band on stage, supporting the band with cash, the venue, the promoters, everyone at work to make the show happen, the security guards whose presence dissuades the worst from occurring tonight. Who knows how many armed interlopers they've fought back at the door? The hordes of extremity kept at bay so we can "enjoy" an hour of idiosyncratic audiovisual entertainment.

A few days before the show I saw a young white homeless guy sitting on an empty storefront step near where I work reading *Blindness* by Jose Saramago. I generally ignore panhandlers in that area who set themselves out at intersections highly trafficked by tourists intent on taking in the old colonial and revolutionary era sites, but this time, passing him reading *Blindness* without asking for money (I'd seen him around recently, always with a book and a little cardboard sign asking for cash), no sign in front of him now, I stopped and knowing that I had spare ones on me, something I rarely have these days, I handed him two dollars and said "Great book." *Blindness* begins with a man in his car suddenly afflicted by a milky white blindness. The blind man is then helped home by a Samaritan who robs him but then soon enough the condition spreads and everyone with it is rounded up in an old hospital until everyone has it, an open symbol for a virus of the existential sort, the spiritual sort, the political sort. I don't raise my fist because I don't want to be afflicted with white blindness. I want to resist viruses of any sort.

Screeching Lady Liberty in a spacesuit of steel. That sums up the singer now, the front man, the master of ceremonies never once uttering yo, yo, yo, or trying to hype the crowd. It's more like witchcraft, warlocking, casting a spell that reminds us of the persistence of evil, its ancient omnipresence, its shamanic evocation in fact a purification ritual, assuming control by summoning, using dissonance to pierce the walls of reality and leech the atmosphere of evil, the way a surgeon opens a body and excises the offending tumor, knowing where it is, how to access it, how to make it visible, and then removing it and closing the wound. It's not satanic evil, not chaotic evil, not the forces of hell unleashed, demons sidewinding through air as though shot from primeval flamethrowers. On the moral continuum the sound assumes a position toward the right, a touch of evil, an alignment or orientation in sync with the great gods of Rock & Roll but also with the blues before it, the tortured holy ghost of those old Robert Johnson recordings, and before that Wagner's *Ring Cycle*, Beethoven, the human spirit in touch with shades and shadows, on the edge of madness, compelled by passion, capable of murder of self and others, the whole history of atrocities, babies tossed into the air and caught on bayonets, sprinting into the wilderness to escape open fields alight with enemy fire, the sturdiest limbs of trees displaying hanged men stripped with skin as cracked and crispy as Peking ducks, or to put it more simply every image you've ever seen of devastation. It's the sound of inanimate wreckage and existential spiritual neuropsychological individual and collective dissolution, unified and simplified and repeated in gusts of sound distorted and enlarged by electricity, the amplifiers like elevated tombstone blocks in Europe, those walls of graves like post-office boxes filled with correspondence from the past in the form of corpses.

What's the equivalent in writing? Is there a neo-medieval lit? I thumb "neo-medieval lit" into my phone and "neo" autocorrects to "bro." Imagine a new church where distorted drop-tuned guitar droning is the music and instead of the bible and hymns it's what? I thumb "need to make a new church," as though I'll get started on it first thing on Sunday morning, take Monday off and concoct sweet PowerPoint proposals, scout locations like ruined churches in the least gentrified parts of the city, start a Kickstarter to raise funds to move the rubble to the middle of a remote forest and design a sound system capable of delivering slow-motion gusts of steel.

The singer wields a handful of small red lasers and moves them around with hands raised like he's holding some indistinct entity animated by the otherworld. The lasers make the stage seem like a UFO landing on your head, that is, if the perspective is vertical instead of horizontal and what's ahead of the crowd is above them instead of in front. There's a crushing aspect to the music, definitely, the sense of something infinitely heavy coming down on our heads, the cumulative water pressure at the bottom of every ocean, the compacting force of airless outerspace. I can't really think of any better way for this to end than for some futuristic touchdown of an amorphous ethereal spaceship coming to abduct us from consternation, anxiety, disbelief, bitterness, whatever else does no one any good, like a stronger magnet pulling a weaker one to itself, attracting heavy metals ingested recently, the poisoning of every real and abstract element of the environment, as though we'd all subsisted on dystopian swordfish steaks, the sense that this could be the coming of the end for the country, that it's somehow occurred on our watch and no one's stopping it, the way you always thought that if you had lived in Nazi Germany you would have undermined the Stormtroopers, and now it seems like it's happening again and what are we doing about it, how are we going to stop it, or will we do nothing and watch it either destroy the world or just as likely undermine and ultimately destroy itself?

The red lasers fade in a mass of gray fog, uncolored by lights above, as the medieval spacecraft of crashing metal and barbed wire and ruined wreckage elevates out of sight and into silence. The lights come up. There will not, of course, be an encore. They're not going to take a piss and smoke a cigarette and then come out and play their big hit for an encore.

My ears ring, the merch table is mobbed, I step outside into foggy new spring air, the sidewalk empty of amalgamated terrorists et cetera. I've lingered outside shows in the past to bum a cigarette and watch everyone spill out of the venue, reenter a world in which their role as audience member no longer defines them, no longer facing the same direction, watching the same movements, listening to the same sounds, their mouths for the most part silent. As audience transforms into individuals again something other than the expected seems possible. I once saw the long-haired Asian bass player for Ariel Pink's Haunted Graffiti deck a heckler, lay him out with a right hook, after their show. The knocked-down guy had been hassling the opening band in which the bass player also played and was thrown out but waited around after the show to confront the bass player. In the end, the heckler's mouth was cut open and bleeding and he seemed disorientated, asking if we'd seen what had happened, looking for witnesses if he pressed charges, but no one took his side.

Tonight I decide to walk it for a while and maybe take a taxi if an unoccupied one passes. The snow has melted but it's still visible in the air, like you can see the new season's breath, its first clear exhalations, the unified front of winter transforming into the individual days of spring. The Center City skyscrapers, illuminated and closer here than where I live, seem like rectangular stumps, as though the air has eroded them from above. I think this is what the city should look like in Trump's America. "Winter in America," the Gil Scott-Heron song, comes to mind. Down alleys, the remaining banks of snow, reduced to receding ice caps, seem like the sleek backs of whales breaching the concrete ocean surface. I stop and take a few photographs I don't upload. The alleys with their weird yellow lighting and shadows, the bricks and concrete, seem to have a life of their own. The edibles are still at work: anthropomorphic vitality I attribute to alleys.

This area is called Eraserhood because David Lynch lived around here when he was a student. He said it informed his later art. Forty years later it's neither horrific nor surreal. Active warehouses, vacant lots, parking lots mixed with warehouses transformed to lofts, a space to cross when headed somewhere else.

There's a narrow concrete corridor under the Convention Center, a somewhat recent construction, completed in the past decade after I moved to town. A bottle smashes nearby but I don't see who threw it. Homeless people tucked under rugs, their possessions covered by tarps, use the tunnel through the Convention Center as a shelter.

I have to start narrating my thoughts like Kali, I think, but then instead of saying it I thumb it into my phone. I haven't been thinking, I haven't been aware, I need to be vigilant.

I walk through Chinatown, bubble tea, unsettled sidewalks, sweet rancid smells, neon lights, the street-level bricks and frontages blackened by exhaust more than elsewhere in the city. The hospital where Kali was born a little more than four years ago, the oldest hospital in America. The block of 10th and Locust, new construction nearby, a block at first I had hoped would be more than it was has over time lived up to its potential with more stores, cafes, restaurants. ACME/Whole Foods restoration well under way at 10th and South Street, more than a decade established. After Bainbridge, a woman in a short skirt, obviously drunk, reels out of an apartment with some friends and looks for an Uber. I note that I've lost a good thought. No idea what it could've been. Something better than just wanting to watch basketball this morning.

On the window of a popular breakfast spot there's a poster that says "Look who's under the hood" with clansmen revealing themselves as Trump and Bannon and friends. "Hate has no home here" placards in so many windows. Before the election this street was 100% in favor of Hillary, there was no way she could lose, and now it's 100% against the new administration. Snow's melting. It feels like a storm has passed.

I step to our stoop and think *it's just pure tone*. I say it aloud, "it's just pure tone," referring to Sunn O))), but it carries more weight than that. The breeze directs a whiff of vetiver from my neck to my nostrils. The light above me in the bathroom toward the back of our long narrow rowhome, its hum the soundtrack for the end of the night. Sixers versus Celtics tomorrow afternoon and then a week of me and Kali alone. Run the credits as the narrator takes a piss and listens to the hum of the overhead bathroom fan, awareness of the sound of electricity for now restored.

Lee Klein is the author of *JRZDVLZ* (Sagging Meniscus), *The Shimmering Go-Between: A Novel* (Atticus Books) and *Thanks + Sorry + Good Luck: Rejection Letters from the Eyeshot Outbox* (Barrelhouse Books), and translator of Horacio Castellanos Moya's *Revulsion: Thomas Bernhard in San Salvador* (New Directions), for which he received a 2015 PEN/Heim Translation Fund Award. He lives in the Philadelphia area with his wife and daughter. Visit litfunforever.com for more.

Printed in the USA
CPSIA information can be obtained
at www.ICGtesting.com
LVHW091826061224
798422LV00006B/1492

* 9 7 8 1 9 4 4 6 9 7 8 2 2 *